William Gillette

Secret service

A Romance of the Southern Confederacy

William Gillette

Secret service
A Romance of the Southern Confederacy

ISBN/EAN: 9783337348359

Printed in Europe, USA, Canada, Australia, Japan

Cover: Foto ©Andreas Hilbeck / pixelio.de

More available books at **www.hansebooks.com**

AN AMERICAN DRAMA
ARRANGED IN FOUR ACTS
AND ENTITLED

SECRET SERVICE

A ROMANCE OF THE
SOUTHERN CONFEDERACY

WRITTEN BY *Horton*
WILLIAM GILLETTE

NEW YORK
SAMUEL FRENCH
PUBLISHER
28-30 WEST 38TH STREET

LONDON
SAMUEL FRENCH, LTD.
26 SOUTHAMPTON STREET
STRAND

CHARACTERS

GENERAL NELSON RANDOLPH.............................
[Commanding in Richmond]

MRS. GENERAL VARNEY...............................
[Wife of a Confederate Officer of High Rank]

EDITH VARNEY..
[Her Daughter]

WILFRED VARNEY......................................
[Her Youngest Son]

CAROLINE MITFORD....................................
From Across the Street]

LEWIS DUMONT..
[United States Secret Service—Known in Richmond as Captain Thorne]

HENRY DUMONT..
[United States Secret Service—Lewis Dumont's Brother]

MR. BENTON ARRELSFORD...............................
[Confederate Secret Service]

MISS KITTRIDGE......................................
[Sewing for the Hospitals]

MARTHA..
[Negro House Servant]

JONAS...
[Negro House Servant]

LIEUT. MAXWELL......................................
[President's Detail]

LIEUT. FORAY..
[First Operator Military Telegraph Lines]

LIEUT. ALLISON......................................
[Second Operator Military Telegraph Lines]

LIEUT. TYREE..
[Artillery]

LIEUT. ENSING.......................................
[Artillery]

SERGEANT WILSON.....................................

SERGEANT ELLINGTON ....

CORPORAL MATSON.....................................

CAVALRY ORDERLY.....................................

ARTILLERY ORDERLY...................................

HOSPITAL MESSENGER..................................

FIRST WAR DEPT. MESSENGER...........................

SECOND WAR DEPT. MESSENGER..........................

THIRD WAR DEPT. MESSENGER...........................

FOURTH WAR DEPT. MESSENGER..........................

TELEGRAPH OFFICE MESSENGER A........................

TELEGRAPH OFFICE MESSENGER B........................

EDDINGER..

AN EVENING IN RICHMOND DURING THE WAR OF THE
REBELLION AT A TIME WHEN THE NORTHERN FORCES
WERE ENTRENCHED BEFORE THE CITY AND ENDEAV-
ORING BY ALL POSSIBLE MEANS TO BREAK DOWN THE
DEFENSES AND CAPTURE THE CONFEDERATE CAPITAL.

* * *

ACT I	DRAWING-ROOM AT GEN. VARNEY'S HOUSE FRANKLIN STREET	EIGHT O'CLOCK
ACT II	THE SAME PLACE	NINE O'CLOCK
ACT III	TELEGRAPH OFFICE WAR DEPARTMENT	TEN O'CLOCK
ACT IV	DRAWING-ROOM AT THE VARNEY HOUSE AGAIN	ELEVEN O'CLOCK

* * *

WHILE NO SPECIAL EFFORT HAS BEEN MADE IN THE
DIRECTION OF HISTORICAL ACCURACY THE MANAGE-
MENT TAKES THE LIBERTY OF REMINDING THE PUB-
LIC THAT THE CITY OF RICHMOND AT THE TIME SET
FORTH IN "SECRET SERVICE" WAS IN A STATE OF
THE UTMOST EXCITEMENT AND CONFUSION. WOUNDED
AND DYING WERE BEING BROUGHT IN FROM THE
DEFENSES BY THE CAR-LOAD. CHURCHES, LIBRARIES
AND PUBLIC BUILDINGS WERE CONVERTED INTO HOS-
PITALS. OWING TO THE SCARCITY OF SURGEONS
AND MEDICAL ATTENDANTS WOMEN AND EVEN YOUNG
GIRLS ASSISTED AT THE DRESSING OF WOUNDS AND
NURSED THE SUFFERERS DAY AND NIGHT. OTHER
WOMEN WERE OCCUPIED SEWING COARSE AND HEAVY
SAND BAGS FOR THE STRENGTHENING OF THE FORTI-
FICATIONS. STRICT MILITARY DISCIPLINE WAS IM-
POSSIBLE. COURTS MARTIAL IF HELD AT ALL WERE
COMPOSED OF ANY AVAILABLE MATERIAL EVEN PRI-
VATE CITIZENS SERVING IF NECESSARY. TROOPS WERE
BEING HURRIED IN FROM THE SOUTH AND NO CARE-

FUL SCRUTINY WAS ATTEMPTED. THIS MADE IT POS-
SIBLE FOR MANY NORTHERN SECRET SERVICE MEN
TO ENTER THE CITY AND REMAIN THERE IN VARIOUS
DISGUISES. IN THE MIDST OF THIS TROUBLE A BRAVE
ATTEMPT AT GAYETY WAS KEPT UP—CHIEFLY BY
THE YOUNG PEOPLE IN A DESPERATE ENDEAVOR TO
DISTRACT THEIR MINDS FROM THE TERRIBLE SITUA-
TION. THERE WERE DANCES AND "STARVATION
PARTIES" SO CALLED BECAUSE OF THE NECESSARILY
LIMITED FARE PROVIDED AND THE BOOMING OF THE
GREAT SIEGE GUNS OFTEN SOUNDED ABOVE THE
STRAINS OF A DREAMY WALTZ OR THE LIVELY BEAT
OF A POLKA.

SECRET SERVICE

Light Plot

ACTS I AND IV—SAME

Foots and 1st Borders: White and Amber Full up.
To work down and up on Cues in Act II.
2 Blue Box Lamps lighting Garden Right.
1 Blue Spot through window 1st E. Right.

ACTS II AND IV

2 Table lamps on scene 1 L. C. Back.
One on desk down stage Right.
These lamps work up and down on Dimmer in Act.
II.
Red Lighting in Garden to flash on backing.
Strip in Back Entrance (Act I only)
Strips in Hallway left and top of stairway to go
out on Cue in Act II.
Lighting works only on sounds of Cannon, Acts II
and IV.

ACT III

4 Telegraph instruments on Scene—2 on table
down center, 2 on table under mantel piece down
right, all to work from off and on stage.
1–2 light (imitation) gas bracket over mantel to go
off and on at Cue.
Foots and 1st Border. White and Amber full up.
To work up and down at Cues.

2 Box lamps green frosted. Showing through windows down stage left, same on all through Act.

Bunches lighting transparency wings back left, cues on Gas Bracket Foots and Border.

Property Plot

Act I

Interior:—Drawing room in General Varney's house; Richmond, Va. 1865. Early evning. Ground-cloth, medallion, rugs—Portieres to draw on L. U. E. Portieres to draw on windows R. and R. C.

On walls:—Handsome pictures in gilt and walnut frames of the period landscapes, steel engravings and portraits.

Furniture:—Colonial mahogany frames and Rep upholstering. Southern Fireplace down L. brass fender, dogs and fireplace furniture.

On Mantel:—Clock—practical set for 8 o'clock. Vases with glass, bronze ornaments, 2 or 3 books. Flowers in grate.

On Table:—L. C. centerpiece, 2 or 3 books, written letter not in envelope. Large plush album. Chair R. and L. of L. C. table) Hassock in front of L. C. table.

Bell cord below F. P.

Sofa R. C. Tidies, sofa cushions.

Table up C. Lighted lamp, work basket fairly large —Pair of scissors, needles, thread, etc. Vase of flowers, one to be removed. Writing desk down R. On desk, writing material, pen, ink and paper, envelopes, etc. Nice old-fashioned ink stand) 2 or 3 books, bowl of flowers, small miniature on easel, waste basket, dark wicker chair in front of desk, chair just above desk, Hassock near desk.

Bookcase between windows and C. doors (old-fashioned, filled with books.)

Stair Carpet.

Hanging Lamp in Hall.

Lamp on desk or small stand R.

Pedestal and vase of flowers between windows—chair
between windows.

Hall seat in hall.

Two chairs, one each side of F. P.

Pedestal and statue on landing in hall.

Vines and flowers for veranda off R. and R. U. E.

SIDE PROPS

For Thorne:—Cigar, matches.

For Jonas:—Writing paper (brown) card, salver, off
L. C.

For Wilfred:—Pair gray Confederate trousers, legs
to cut off about three inches from bottom every
night. Confederate gray blouse wrapped in
brown paper.

For Edith:—(Upstairs L. C.) written note.

For Maxwell:—Large official brown envelope containing commission.

For Miss Kittridge:—(Off C.) Package of lint and
package of bandages.

For Soldier:—Sling.

8 Springfield rifles and bayonets.

Jingle door bell off L. C.

Distant cannon effect off R.

Effect of passing artillery off R. rumble of cannon
wheels, horses galloping, and jingle of swords
and harness. Door slam (big) off L. C. See
that key is in lock of C. door and that it will
work easily.

ACT II

SAME SET AS ACT I

Set clock at 9 o'clock.

SIDE PROPS

For Wilfred:—Lot of papers, letters, etc. 1 letter partly written not in envelope.

For Martha:—Off L. 3, large official brown envelope.

For Mrs. Varney:—Off L. C. (at top of stairs) Wilfred's cap and belt, roll of gray blankets tied, open written letter.

For Arrelsford:—Same paper taken from Jonas, Act I.

For Thorne:—Sure fire army revolver in holster.

ACT III

Interior:—The War Department Telegraph Office. Groundcloth, to represent board floor. Wide mantel shelf and fireplace down R. Front of fireplace plain solid table rather long and narrow. On table, 4 telegraph instruments of the period 1865, connected each separately to sounder and key off stage R. Pens, inkwells, paper (manila), telegraph-blanks (form used by Confederate war department), spindles, etc.

On wall:—Above mantel Rough hooks to hang coats on.

On mantel:—Piles of old messages and books.

Plain solid table R. C. fastened firmly to floor.

On table:—2 telegraph instruments of the period connected each separately off stage R.

Paper, pens, ink, telegraph forms of the period.

Small cup about the size of a sponge cup sunk in table and containing sponge and carmine for Captain Thorne's bloody hand business. Pot of paste and brush.

Revolver on shelf of table. The Telegraph wires from these instruments on both tables drop down to floor in full view of audience and carried across and out through upper part of fireplace to table off stage. Where each instrument on stage is connected to an instrument off stage; have off stage instruments all on one table; the ones for the long table near F. P. are lettered B. and C. those on the table R. C., lettered A. and D. frm the top of the F. P. fake wires run up side of scene to ceiling and across stage to center window, out of that window and up out of sight; have large glass insulators such as were used then to carry wires.

2 Common chairs at long table R.

1 Common chair at table R. C.

1 Chair up C.

Waste paper basket full of waste paper R. C.

In Closet up C.:—Shelves containing battery jars and rubbish natural to a telegraph office. Boxes —Rubbish, etc. Have lot of battery jars under table in front of F. P. with proper connections (faked).

Big double break away doors up R. C. These have big iron bar and cleats on audience side. These doors must be very solid and are practically smashed to bits each performance with butts of guns hinges in down stage one should break away.

If windows L. are not real glass have glass crash effect off L. supposed to be breaking of glass when shot is fired through window.

Lot of waste paper (old despatches on floor).

SIDE PROPS

For Thorne:—Sure fire revolver, official order, official despatch, cigar, matches.

For Edith:—Official commission.

For Caroline:—Official order.

For Eddinger:—Official order.

For Arrelsford:—Official order, sure fire revolver.

For Messenger:—1 Official despatch.

For Messenger:—4 Official despatches.

For S. M.:—Sure fire revolver.

8 Springfield rifles and bayonets.

Act IV

SAME SETS AS ACTS I AND II

Furniture slightly disarranged as is left after disturbance of Act II.

Distant cannon effect off R.

Distant musketry effect off R.

Loud bomb shell effects and flashes; hurried and violent ringing of alarm in distance off R. deep low tone like fire bell (Get as near as possible tone of bell used for purpose in Richmond).

4 Big toned chimes. .

Effects of cavalry, artillery, etc., passing horses' hoofs, rattling of sabers and gun carriages, chain effect off R., crunching effect on gravel road. (All the above on cues both very distant and close).

SIDE PROPS

For Thorne:—Fuller's-earth, dark cloth for bandage, revolver.

For Wilfred:—White neck bandage, fuller's-earth.

For Mrs. Varney:—Ladies' linen handkerchief.

For Jonas:—Springfield cartridge with bullet; separate bullet.

For Orderly:—Fuller's-earth.

For Soldier:—Off L. small basin of water and cloth.

For 8 Soldiers:—Dummy Springfield cartridges, powder removed but bullets put back in their cartridge-boxes.

EFFECTS DURING THE PLAY:—*At intervals while the First and Second Acts of this piece are in progress occasional distant thunder of cannon with flashes, etc., and arrange not to interfere with dialogue or scenes. During Last Act, at periods arranged, the artillery effects become stronger as a desperate attack is then being made upon the Confederate Lines near the Outskirts of the City. But even then these effects should be subdued and distant. The Fortification Lines are from 5 to 10 miles out.*

During First and Fourth Acts—on cues—the passing of regiments hurriedly through the streets outside. Clatter of hoofs, tramp of many feet, rattle of gun-carriages, bugle calls, orders shouted, etc.

Memorandum on Dialect

In several of the Characters "Ah" is used in the place of "I". This does not signify that it should be pronounced as written. It is only to serve as a reminder that the Southern pronunciation is a trifle away from "I" and toward "Ah"—but not by any means reaching it.

SECRET SERVICE

ACT I

SCENE:—*Drawing-room in General Varney's House —Franklin Street—Richmond.*

<u>EIGHT O'CLOCK</u>

A richly furnished room.—Southern characteristics.

Fire-place on left side. Wide doors or arch up left set diagonally open to a front hall. Portieres on these doors or arch to draw completely closing opening. Stairway seen through these doors or arch, in the hall, at back, ascending from a landing a few steps high back of center of opening, and rising off to L. Entrance to street off L. below stairs. Entrance to dining room and kitchen off R. below stairs. Both of these openings are back of double doors or arch up L. C. Wide door at center opening to a back parlor which is being used for women who come there to sew and work for hospitals. In elaborate production these women are seen in the room at back seated at tables working, when the doors are opened. Two double French windows on right side, one up stage set oblique, and one down, both opening to a wide veranda. Shrubbery, etc., beyond the veranda and vines, etc., on balustrade and posts of veranda—which must be in line of sight for whole house outside the upper of these two windows. Both these windows are " French " extending down to floor,

13

and to open and close on hinges. They also have curtains or draperies which can easily be drawn to cover them. Below window down R. a writing desk and chair. Between these windows and pedestal and vase of flowers to be knocked over by THORNE in ACT IV. Chair near pedestal—chair and cabinet R. of C. door against wall. Table L. of C. door against wall with lamp and vase of flowers. Couch R. C. Table and 2 chairs L. C. Chair each side of F. P. Left. Hall seat in hall. Pedestal and statue on landing in hall. Dark or nearly dark outside windows R. with strong moonlight effect. Lights on in hall outside door up Left and in room up Center, but not glaring—Light in the room itself full on but shaded so that it gives subdued effect. No fire in fire-place L. Portieres on both windows closed at rise, windows closed at rise.

(At rise of curtain low distant boom of cannonading rolls in distance and quiets down—then is heard again.)

(MISS KITTRIDGE, one of the women who are sewing for the hospitals, enters C. D. comes down C. a little—stops, listens to the sound of cannon —with a worried look—crosses to window up R. looks out. Flashes on her face, then turns and goes down toward table at L. C.—She gathers up pieces of cloth and linen rags that are on the table, looks toward window again, then takes them off at door up C. closing the door carefully after her)

(Sounds of a heavy door closing outside L.)

(Enter at door up L. WILFRED VARNEY, a handsome boy of about sixteen or seventeen—impetuous— Southern—black-eyed—dark hair. He is fairly

well dressed, but in a suit of clothes that has evidently been worn some time. Nothing new or "swell" about it. Dark shade. He has a determined look on his face, and comes rapidly into the room looking about. He goes to door up C. opens it a little way and looks off. Closes it. Goes to window up R. Throws open portieres and windows and looks anxiously off. Red flashes on backing. Distant boom and low thunder of cannon.)

(*Enter* MARTHA, *a negro servant up* L. *coming from door at foot of stairs.* WILFRED *turning sees her, and crosses toward her.*)

WILFRED.   Where's mother?

MARTHA.   She's up staars with Mars Howard sah.

WILFRED.   Ah've got to see 'er!

MARTHA.   Mars Howard he's putty bad dis ebenin' —Ah dunno's she'd want to leave 'im.—Ah'll go up an' see what she says. (*Exit door up* L. *and up the stairway*)

(WILFRED *left alone moves restlessly about, especially when low rumble of distant cannon is heard. Effect of passing artillery in the street outside. On hearing it he hurries to the window and looks out, continuing to do so while the sounds of the passing guns, horses and men are heard. While he is at the window* R. MRS. VARNEY *enters, coming down the stairway and on at door up left. She is quiet, pale, with white or nearly white hair and a rather young face. Her dress is black and though rich, is plain. Not in the least "dressy" or fashionable.—In manner she is calm and self-possessed. She pauses and looks at* WILFRED *a moment. He turns and sees her.* MARTHA *follows her down and exits door at foot of stairway.*)

WILFRED. (*goes toward her—She meeting him* C.) Howard isn't worse is he?

Mrs. Varney. Ah'm afraid so.

Wilfred. Anything Ah can do?

Mrs. Varney. (*shakes head*) No—no.—We can only wait—and hope. (Wilfred *walks away a little as if he could not quite say the thing on his mind*) Ah'm thankful there's a lull in the cannonading. Do they know why it stopped? (*boom of cannon— a low distant rumble*)

Wilfred. (r. c.) It hasn't stopped altogether— don't you hear?

Mrs. Varney. (c.) Yes, but compared to what it was yesterday—you know it shook the house—and Howard suffered dreadfully! (Wilfred *suddenly faces her*)

Wilfred. (r. c.) So did I mother! (*slight pause*) (*low boom of cannon*)

Mrs. Varney. (c.) You!

Wilfred. (r. c.) When Ah hear those guns and know the fighting's on, it makes me——

Mrs. Varney. (*goes toward table* l. c. *Interrupting quickly*) Yes, yes—we all suffered—we all suffered, dear! (*sits* r. *of table* l. c.)

Wilfred. Mother, Ah want to speak to you! You may not like it but you must listen—you must let me —(*goes toward her*)

Mrs. Varney. (*motioning so that he stops. Slight pause. She soon speaks in a low voice. She takes his hand in a motherly way*) I know—what it is.

Wilfred. (l. c.) Ah can't stay back here any longer! It's worse than being shot to pieces! Ah can't do it mother! (Mrs. Varney *looks steadily into* Wilfred's *face but says nothing. Soon she turns away a little as if she felt tears coming into her eyes*) Why don't you speak?

Mrs. Varney. (*turning to him. A faint attempt to smile*) Ah don't know what to say.

Wilfred. Say you won't mind if Ah go down there and help 'em!

MRS. VARNEY. It wouldn't be true!

WILFRED. I can't stay here!

MRS. VARNEY. You're so young Wilfred!

WILFRED. No younger than Tom Kittridge—no younger than Ell Stuart—nor cousin Stephen—nor hundreds of the fellows fighting down there!— See mother—they've called for all over nineteen—that was weeks ago! The eighteen call may be out any minute—the next one after that takes me! Do I want to stay back here till they order me out! Ah should think not! (*walks about to* C. *Stops and speaks to* MRS. VARNEY) If Ah was hit with a shell an' had to stay it would be different! But Ah can't stand this—Ah can't do it mother!

MRS. VARNEY. (*rising and going to him. After pause—Turns as if she were giving way to him*) I'll write to your father.

WILFRED. Why that'll take forever! You don't know where his Division is—they change 'em every day! I can't wait for you to write.

MRS. VARNEY. (*shakes her head.—Speaks finally*) I couldn't let you go without his consent! You must be patient! (WILFRED *starts slowly toward door* L. *with head lowered in disappointment,—but not ill-naturedly.* MRS. VARNEY *looks yearningly after him a moment as he moves away, then goes toward him*) Wilfred! (WILFRED *turns and meets her and she holds him and smooths his hair a little with her hand*) Don't feel bad that you have to stay here with your mother a little longer!

WILFRED. Aw—It isn't that!

MRS. VARNEY. My darling boy—I know it! You want to fight for your country—and I'm proud of you! I want my sons to do their duty! But with your father commanding a brigade at the front and one boy lying wounded—perhaps mortally— (*pause.* MRS. VARNEY *moves away a few steps toward* R.)

WILFRED. (*after pause—goes to her*) Well you'll write to father to-night—won't you?

MRS. VARNEY. Yes—yes! (*door bell is heard ringing in distant part of the house.* WILFRED *and* MRS. VARNEY *both listen.*—MARTHA *crosses outside door up* L. *from* R. *on her way to open the front door. Heavy sound of door off* L. *In a moment she returns and appears at door up* L.)

MARTHA. Hit's one o' de men fum de hossiple ma'am. (WILFRED *hurries to door up* L. *and exits to see the messenger*)

MRS. VARNEY. We've just sent all the bandages we have.

MARTHA. He says de's all used up, an' two more trains juss come in crowded full o' wounded sojers—an' mos' all of 'em drefful bad!

MRS. VARNEY. Is Miss Kittridge here yet?

MARTHA. Yaas'm.

MRS. VARNEY. Ask her if they've got enough to send. Even if it's only a little, let them have it. What they need most is bandages.

MARTHA. (*crossing toward door up* C.) Yaas'm. (*exits door up* C. MRS. VARNEY *goes toward the door up* L. *Stops near the door and speaks a word to* MESSENGER *who is waiting at front door, to attract his attention—then beckons him*)

MRS. VARNEY. Oh— (*beckoning*) Come in. (*she moves toward* C. MESSENGER *appears at the door up* L. *He is a cripple soldier in battered Confederate uniform.—His arm. is in a sling*) What hospital did you come from?

MESSENGER. (*remains up near door* L.) The Winder, ma'am.

MRS. VARNEY. Have you been to St. Paul's? You know the ladies are working there to-night.

MESSENGER. Yes—but they hain't a-workin' for the hospitals, mam—they're making sandbags for the fortifications.

MRS. VARNEY. Well, I hope we can give you something. (MISS KITTRIDGE *enters at door up* C.

bringing a small bundle of lint, etc. MRS. VARNEY *moves down* R. C.)

MISS KITTRIDGE. This is all there is now. (*She hands the package to the* MESSENGER) If you'll come back in an hour, we'll have more for you. (MESSENGER *takes package and exits door* L. *Sound of front door closing outside* L.) We're all going to stay to-night, Miss Varney. There's so many more wounded come in it won't do to stop now.

MRS. VARNEY. (*on sofa*) No, no—we mustn't stop.

MISS KITTRIDGE. (*up* L. C.) Is—is your son—is there any change?

MRS. VARNEY. Ah'm afraid the fever's increasing.

MISS KITTRIDGE. Has the Surgeon seen him this evening?

MRS. VARNEY. No—oh, no! (*shaking her head*) We couldn't ask him to come twice—with so many waiting for him at the hospital.

MISS KITTRIDGE. But they couldn't refuse *you* Mrs. Varney! (*a sudden idea*) There's that man going right back to the hospital! I'll call him and send word that—(*starting toward the door* L. *to do so*)

MRS. VARNEY. (*detaining her*) No no—I can't let you! (*rises—goes toward her a step*)

MISS KITTRIDGE. Not for—your own son?

MRS. VARNEY. Think how many sons must be entirely neglected to visit mine twice! (*sound of door outside* L.—*Enter* EDITH VARNEY—*a light quick entrance—coming from outside—hat in hand as if just taking it off as she enters*)

MRS. VARNEY. Edith dear! How late you are! You must be tired out!

EDITH. (*shaking head*) Ah'm not tired at all! Besides, I haven't been at the hospital all day. Goodbye, Miss Kittridge! I want to tell Mama something.

MISS KITTRIDGE. O dear! I'll get out of hearing right quick! (*exit at door up* C.)

EDITH. (*up to door lightly and calling after* MISS KITTRIDGE) I hope you don't mind!

MISS KITTRIDGE. (*as she exits up* C.) Mercy, no! (EDITH *closes the door and goes to* MRS. VARNEY *taking her down stage to chair* R. *of table.* MRS. VARNEY *sits in chair and* EDITH *on stool close to her on her* L. *in front of table* L. C.)

EDITH. Mama—what do you think? What *do* you think?

MRS. VARNEY. What is it, dear?

EDITH. Ah've been to see the President!

MRS. VARNEY. What!—Mr. Davis!

EDITH. Yes! An' Ah asked him for an appointment for Captain Thorne for the War Department Telegraph Service—an' he gave it to me—a Special Commission! Appointing him to duty here in Richmond—a very important position—so now he won't have to be sent back to the front—an' it'll be doing his duty just the same.

MRS. VARNEY. But Edith—you don't——

EDITH. Yes it will, Mama! The President told me they needed a man who understood telegraphing and who was of high enough rank to take charge of the Service! And you know Cap'n Thorne is an expert! Since he's been here in Richmond he's helped 'em in the telegraph office very often— Lieutenant Foray told me so! (MRS. VARNEY *slowly rises and moves away toward* C.—*After a slight pause*) Now, Mama, Ah feel you're going to scold —an' you mustn't because it's all fixed, an' the commision'll be sent over here in a few minutes—just as soon as it can be made out! An' the next time he comes Ah'm to hand it to him myself. (*crosses down* L.)

MRS. VARNEY. (*moves toward table*) He's coming this evening.

EDITH. (*looks at* MRS. VARNEY *an instant before speaking.—Then in low voice*) How do you know?

MRS. VARNEY. (*going back of table*) This note came half an hour ago. (*about to hand note from table to* EDITH.—EDITH *sees note and anticipates her action—picking it up and going quickly* R. *with it*)

EDITII. Has it been here—all this time? (*she sits on divan* R. *and opens envelope eagerly, and reads note*)

MRS. VARNEY. (*after a moment*) You see what he says? This'll be his last call.—He's got his orders to leave. (*sits* R. *of table* L. C.)

EDITII. (*sitting on divan* R. C.) Why, it's too ridiculous! Just as if the commission from the President wouldn't supersede everything? It puts him at the head of the Telegraph Service! He'll be in the command of the Department!—He says— (*glancing at note*) good-by call does he! All the better—it'll be that much more of a surprise! (*rising and going toward* MRS. VARNEY) Now Mama, don't you breathe—Ah want to tell him myself!

MRS. VARNEY. But Edith dear—Ah don't quite approve of your going to the President about this.

EDITII. (*changing from light manner to earnestness*) But listen, Mama—Ah couldn't go to the War Department people—Mr. Arrelsford's there in one of the offices—and ever since Ah refused him you know how he's treated me!—(*slight deprecatory motion from* MISS VARNEY) If Ah'd applied for the appointment there he'd have had it refused— and he'd have got them to order Cap'n Thorne away right off—Ah know he would—and—(*stands motionless as she thinks of it*) That's where his orders to go came from!

MRS. VARNEY. But my dear——

EDITII. It is, Mama! (*slight pause*) Isn't it

lucky I got that commission to-day! (*Emphasis on "Isn't." Crossing down* R.—*at* R. C. *near lounge*) (*door bell rings in distant part of the house,*—JONAS *goes across hall to the door up* L.—MRS. VARNEY *moves up stage a little waiting to see who it is.*— EDITH *listening.*—*Heavy sound of door off* L.— JONAS *enters at the door up* L.)

JONAS. (*coming down* R. *of* MRS. VARNEY) It's a officer, ma'am.   He says he's fum de President—an —(*hands a card to* MRS. VARNEY) he's got ter see Miss Edith pussonully.

EDITH. (*going up* C. *a little. Low voice*) It's come, Mama!

MRS. VARNEY. (*rises and goes up* C. *toward* EDITH) Ask the gentleman in.   (*hands card to* EDITH. JONAS *exits at door up* L.)

EDITH. (*overjoyed but keeping voice low*) It's the commission!

MRS. VARNEY. (*low voice*) Do you know who it is? (*showing* EDITH *the card*)

EDITH. (*glances at card. Low voice*) No! But he's from the President—it must be that!

(*Enter* JONAS *at door up* L.   *He comes on a little bowing someone in.*)

(*Enter* LIEUT. MAXWELL *at door up* L.—*He is a very dashing young officer, handsome, polite and dressed in a showy and perfectly fitting uniform.* JONAS *exits at up* L.   MRS. VARNEY *advances a little.*)

LIEUT. MAXWELL.   Good evening.   (*bowing*) (MRS. VARNEY *and* EDITH *bow slightly.   To* MRS. VARNEY) Have Ah the honah of addressing Miss Varney?

MRS. VARNEY. (C.)   I am Mrs. Varney, sir. (*emphasizing "Mrs." a little*)

LIEUT. MAXWELL. (L. C.   *Bowing to* MRS.

VARNEY) Madam—Ah'm very much afraid this looks like an intrusion on my part, but Ah come from the President and he desires me to see Miss Varney personally!

MRS. VARNEY. Anyone from the President could not be otherwise than welcome.—This is my daughter. (*indicating* EDITH *who is* R. C.)

(LIEUT. MAXWELL *bows to* EDITH *and she returns the salutation. He then walks across to her, taking a large brown envelope from his belt.*)

LIEUT. MAXWELL. Miss Varney, the President directed me to deliver this into your hands—with his compliments. (*handing it to* EDITH) He is glad to be able to do this not only at your request, but as a special favor to your father, General Varney.

EDITH. (*taking envelope*) Oh, thank you! (*goes down* R. C. *a little*)

MRS. VARNEY. Won't you be seated, Lieutenant?

EDITH. (*in front of couch* R. C.) O yes—do! (*holds envelope pressed very tight against her side*)

LIEUT. MAXWELL. (*down* C.) Nothing would please me so much, ladies—but Ah have to be back at the President's house right away. Ah'm on duty this evening.—Would you mind writing me off a line or two, Miss Varney—just to say you have the communication?

EDITH. Why certainly—(*takes a step or two toward desk at right*) You want a receipt—I—(*turns and crosses toward door up* L.) I'll go upstairs to my desk—it won't take a moment! (*turns at door*) And—could I put in how much I thank him for his kindness?

LIEUT. MAXWELL. (C.) Ah'm sure he'd be more than pleased! (EDITH *exits at door up* L. *and hastens up the stairway outside* L.)

MRS. VARNEY. (*moving forward slowly*) We

haven't heard so much cannonading to-day, Lieutenant. Do they know what it means?

LIEUT. MAXWELL. (*going forward with* MRS.
VARNEY) Ah don't think they're quite positive,
ma'am, but they can't help lookin' for a violent attack
to follow.

MRS. VARNEY. I don't see why it should quiet
down before an assault!

LIEUT. MAXWELL. (*near* c.) It might be some
signal, ma'am, or it might be they're moving their
batteries to open on a special point of attack. They're
tryin' ev'ry way to break through our defenses you
know.

(*Door bell rings in distant part of house.*)

MRS. VARNEY. It's very discouraging! (*seats
herself* R. *of table* L. c.) We can't seem to drive
them back this time!

LIEUT. MAXWELL. We're holding 'em where they
are though! They'll never get in unless they do it
by some scurvy trick—that's where the danger lies!
(*heavy sound of door off* L.)

(*Enter* EDITH *coming lightly and quickly down the
stairway up* L. *As* EDITH *speaks* MAXWELL *goes
up* c. *a little to meet her.*)

EDITH. (*entering, with a note in her hand, and
without the official envelope, which she has left in
her room upstairs*) Is Lieutenant Maxwell—(*Seeing him down stage with* MRS. VARNEY *and going
across toward him*) O yes!

(JONAS *enters at door up* L. *as* EDITH *reaches up* c.,
showing in CAPTAIN THORNE.)

JONAS. (*as he enters. Low voice*) Will you jess
kinely step dis way, suh!

(MRS. VARNEY *rises and moves down in front of
and then up* L. *of table.* MAXWELL *turns and
meets* EDITH *up* R. c.)

EDITH. (*meeting* MAXWELL *up* R. C.)   I didn't know but you—(*she stops—hearing* JONAS *up* L. *and quickly turns, looking off* L.)   Oh!—Captain Thorne!

(*Enter* CAPTAIN THORNE *at door up* L. *meeting and shaking hands with* EDITH *nearly up* C.— CAPTAIN THORNE *is dressed as a Confederate Captain of Artillery. His uniform is somewhat worn and soiled.* LIEUT. MAXWELL *turned and moved up a little on* EDITH'S *entrance, remaining a little* R. *of* C. JONAS *exits up* L. C.)

EDITH. (*up* C. *Giving* THORNE *her hand briefly*) We were expecting you!—Here's Captain Thorne, mama!

(MRS. VARNEY *moves up* L. *meeting* THORNE *up* L. C. *and shaking hands with him graciously.*— EDITH *turns away and goes to* LIEUT. MAXWELL *up* R. C.—THORNE *and* MRS. VARNEY *move up* C. *near small table and converse, well up out of the way.*)

EDITH. (R. C. *Going to* LIEUT. MAXWELL) I wasn't so very long writing it, was I Lieutenant? (*she hands* LIEUT. MAXWELL *the note she has written to the President*)

LIEUT. MAXWELL. (*up* R. C.)   Ah've never seen a quicker piece of work, Miss Varney. (*putting note in belt or pocket*)   When you want a clerkship ovah at the Government offices you must shorely let me know!

EDITH. (*smilingly*)   You'd better not commit yourself—Ah might take you at your word!

LIEUT. MAXWELL.   Nothing would please me so much Ah'm sure!   All you've got to do is just to apply!

EDITH.   Lots of the girls are doing it—they have to, to live!   Aren't there a good many where you are?

LIEUT. MAXWELL. Well we don't have so many as they do over at the Treasury. Ah believe there are more ladies there than men!

MRS. VARNEY. (*comes down a little*) Perhaps you gentlemen have met!—(*glancing toward* LIEUT. MAXWELL)

(THORNE *shakes head a little and steps forward* L. C. *looking at* MAXWELL.)

MRS. VARNEY. (*introducing*) Cap'n Thorne— Lieutenant Maxwell.

THORNE. (*slight inclination of head*) Lieutenant.

LIEUT. MAXWELL. (*returning bow pleasantly*) I haven't had that pleasure—though Ah've heard the Cap'n's name mentioned several times!

THORNE. Yes? (MRS. VARNEY *and* EDITH *are looking at* MAXWELL *cheerfully*)

LIEUT. MAXWELL. (*as if it were rather amusing*) In fact Cap'n, there's a gentleman in one of our offices who seems mighty anxious to pick a fight with you!

(EDITH *is suddenly serious and a look of apprehension spreads over* MRS. VARNEY's *face.*)

THORNE. (*easily*) Pick a fight! Really! Why what office is that, Lieutenant?

LIEUT. MAXWELL. (*slightly annoyed*) The War Office, sir!

THORNE. Dear, dear! Ah didn't suppose you had anybody in the War Office who wanted to fight!

LIEUT. MAXWELL. (*almost angry*) An' why not, sir?

THORNE. (*easily*) Well if he did he'd hardly be in an office would he—at a time like this?

LIEUT. MAXWELL. (*trying to be light again*) Ah'd better not tell him that, Cap'n—he'd certainly insist on havin' you out!

THORNE. (*moving down* L. C. *with* MRS. VARNEY)

That would be too bad—to interfere with the gentleman's office hours! (THORNE *and* MRS. VARNEY *move down* L. C. *near table—in conversation*)

LIEUT. MAXWELL. (*to* EDITH) He doesn't believe it, Miss Varney,—but it's certainly true, an' I dare say you know who the——

EDITH. (*quickly interrupting* MAXWELL—*low voice*) Please don't Lieutenant!—I—(*an apprehensive glance toward* THORNE) I'd rather not—(*with a slight catch of breath*)—talk about it!

LIEUT. MAXWELL. (*after short pause of surprise*) Yes, of course!—Ah didn't know there was any——

EDITH. (*interrupting again, with attempt to turn it off*) Yes! (*a rather nervous effort to laugh lightly*)—You know there's always the weather to fall back on!

LIEUT. MAXWELL. (*picking it up easily*) Yes— Ah should say so! An' mighty bad weather too— most of the time!

EDITH. (*laughingly*) Yes—isn't it! (*they laugh a little and go on talking and laughing to themselves, moving toward* R. *upper window for a moment and soon move across toward door up* L. *as if* MAXWELL *were going*)

MRS. VARNEY. (*back of table* L. C., R. *of* THORNE) From your note Captain Thorne, I suppose you're leaving us soon. Your orders have come.

THORNE. (*back of table* L. C. L. *of* MRS. VARNEY) Yes—Mrs. Varney they have.—Ah'm afraid this'll be my last call.

MRS. VARNEY. Isn't it rather sudden? It seems to me they ought to give you a little time.

THORNE. Ah well (*slight smile*) we have to be ready for anything you know!

MRS. VARNEY. (*with a sigh*) Yes—I know!—It's been a great pleasure to have you drop in on us while you were here. We shall quite miss your visits.

THORNE. (*a slight formality in manner*) Thank

you. I shall never forget what they've been to me.

(MAXWELL *is taking leave of* EDITH *up* C.)

EDITH. (*up* C.)   Lieutenant Maxwell is going, Mama!

MRS. VARNEY. So soon! Excuse me a moment, Captain! (*goes hurriedly toward* MAXWELL.—THORNE *goes down* L. *of table* L. C. *near mantel*) Ah'm right sorry to have you hurry away, Lieutenant. We shall hope for the pleasure of seeing you again. (R. *of* MAXWELL)

LIEUT. MAXWELL. Ah shall certainly call, Mrs. Varney—if you'll allow me.—Cap'n! (*saluting* THORNE *from near door up* L.)

THORNE. (*turning from mantel. Half salute*) Lieutenant!

MAXWELL. Miss Varney! Mrs. Varney! (*bowing to each. Exits door up* L. MRS. VARNEY *follows* MAXWELL *off at door up* L.—*speaking as she goes*)

(THORNE *turns to book or something on table* L. C. *after saluting* MAXWELL.)

MRS. VARNEY. (*as she goes off with* MAXWELL) Now remember Lieutenant, you're to come sometime when duty doesn't call you away so soon!

(EDITH *turns and moves slowly to table up* C. *on* MAXWELL'S *exit*)

LIEUT. MAXWELL. (*outside.—Voice getting more distant*)   Trust me to attend to that, Mrs. Varney!

(EDITH *at small table up* C.—*After a little pause* THORNE *looks toward her. Heavy sound of door off* L.)

THORNE. (*moving up a little toward* EDITH *who is up* C. *near small table*)   Shall I see Mrs. Varney again?

EDITH. (*getting a rose from vase on table up* L. C.

Turning at table up L. C.) Oh yes—you'll see her again!—But not just now. (*she moves down* C. *a little coming even with* THORNE *who is* L. *of her*)

THORNE. I haven't long to stay.

EDITH. (*moving down* C. *a little.* THORNE *moves with her to back of table*) Oh—not long!

THORNE. (*as he moves down with her*) No—I'm sorry to say.

EDITH. (*down* C. *a little*) Well—do you know— Ah think you have more time than you really think you have! It would be odd if it came out that way —wouldn't it? (*playing with flower in her hand*)

THORNE. Yes—but it won't come out that way.

EDITH. Yes—but you—(*she stops as* THORNE *is taking the rose from her hand—which she was holding up in an absent way as she talked.* THORNE *at the same time holds the hand she had it in. She lets go of the rose and draws away her hand*)

(*Slight pause.*)

EDITH. (*a little embarrassed*) You know—you can sit down if you want to! (*indicating chair at* L. *of table*)

THORNE. Yes—I see.

EDITH. (*sits* R. *of table* L. C.) You'd better!— Oh, I've a great many things to say!

THORNE. Oh—you have!

EDITH. (*nodding.—Her left hand is on the table*) Yes.

THORNE. I have only one.

EDITH. (*looking up at him*) And—that is—?

THORNE. (*taking her* L. *hand in both of his*) Good-bye.

EDITH. But Ah don't really think you'll have to say it!

THORNE. (*looking tenderly down at her*) I know I will!

EDITH. (*low voice—more serious*) Then it'll be because you want to!

THORNE. (*quickly leaning forward and down to her*) No! It will be—because I must.

EDITH. (*rising slowly and looking at him a little mischievously as she does so*) Oh—because you must! (THORNE *nods a little—saying " yes " with his lips.* EDITH *walks towards* C. *thinking whether to tell him or not.—He watches her.—She suddenly turns back and goes again to table* L. C. *Leaning toward him a little over the table*) You don't know some things I do!

THORNE. (*laughing a little first*) Ah think that's more than likely, Miss Varney! (THORNE *goes to* L. *of table* L. C.) Would you mind telling me a few so Ah can somewhat approach you in that respect?

EDITH. (R. *of table* L. C. *Seriously*) Ah wouldn't mind telling you one, and that is, it's very wrong for you to think of leaving R'chmond yet!

THORNE. Ah—but you don't——

EDITH. (*sits in chair* R. *of table* L. C. *Breaking in quickly*) Oh, yes, Ah do!

THORNE. (*sits in chair* L. *of table* L. C. *Looking up at her amused*) Well—what?

EDITH. Whatever you were going to say! Most likely it was that there's something or other Ah don't know about!—But Ah know this—(*looking away front—eyes lowered a little*) you were sent here only a few weeks ago to recover from a very bad wound—(THORNE *looks down and a little front quickly, a sudden expression of pain on his face*)—and you haven't nearly had time for it yet!

THORNE. (*as if amused*) Ha ha—yes. (*looking up at* EDITH, *with usual expression*) Ah do look as if the next high wind would blow me away, don't I?

EDITH. (*turning to him earnestly—half rising*) No matter how you look, you ought not—Oh—(*rising fully and turning away from him*) You're just making fun of it, like you always do! (*goes up* C. *to near table.—Turns to* THORNE *again*) No matter!

You can make all the fun you like, but the whole thing is settled, and you aren't going away at all!

(THORNE *has risen when* EDITH *did.*)

THORNE. Oh—Ah'm not!

EDITH. No!

THORNE. Well, that's quite a change for me! (*puts hat on table and moves up near* EDITH *going back of table*) Perhaps you wouldn't mind telling me what I am going to do?

EDITH. (*up* C. *a little. Turning to him*) Ah wouldn't mind at all—an' it's this—you see Ah've been to the—(*hesitates*) Now! Ah'm almost afraid to tell you!

THORNE. (*near* EDITH—*left of her*) Don't tell me Miss Varney—because it's really true. I've got my orders—I'm leaving to-night.

(EDITH *looks at* THORNE *an instant—then turns and goes* R. *and sits on lounge or ottoman, looking at him from there.*)

EDITH. (*after looking at* THORNE *an instant*) Where—to the front?

(THORNE *moves over to* EDITH R.)

THORNE. We can't always tell where orders'll take us. (*he sits on the lounge beside her—on her left*)

EDITH. (*after* THORNE *is seated near her*) But listen! Supposing there were other orders—from a higher authority—appointing you to duty here?

THORNE. (*eyes lowered before him*) It wouldn't make any difference.

EDITH. (*sudden alarm*) You don't—you don't mean you'd go—in spite of them? (THORNE *raises his eyes to hers in slight surprise at her sudden earnestness, and looks at her an instant. Then he nods affirmatively*) But if it proved your first order was a mistake—and—(*in her earnestness she makes a little motion with her left hand within his reach*)

THORNE. (*taking her hand in his*) It wasn't a mistake (*they look at one another.—He hesitates, Looks down before him.—Looks up in her face an instant—then releasing her hand rises and moves up* R. C. *a little standing faced up toward window*)

(*After watching* THORNE *until he is motionless* EDITH *rises and comes up* C. *to* L. *of him.*)

EDITH. (*up* C. *With a new apprehension*) Is it— something dangerous?

THORNE. (*up* R. C. *Turning to* EDITH *and speaking lightly*) Oh, well—(*slight laugh*) enough to make it interesting!

EDITH. (*low voice*) Don't be angry if I ask you again about your orders—I must know!

THORNE. Why?

EDITH. No matter—tell me!

THORNE. (*slight shake of head*) I can't do that Miss Varney.

EDITH. You needn't! Ah know! (THORNE *a sudden apprehensive glance to front. Looks back to her at once*) They're sending you on some mission where death is almost certain. They'll sacrifice your life because they know you are fearless and will do anything! There's a chance for you to stay here and be just as much use—and Ah'm going to ask you to do this! It isn't your life alone—there are other lives to think of—that's why I ask you!—It may not sound well—but—you see——

THORNE. (*catching her hands passionately*) Ah my—(*suddenly recovering and partly turning away —not, however, releasing her hands*) No no!— You shan't have this against me too!

EDITH. Against you! Why? Why? What do you mean? Why is it against you?

THORNE. (*holding her hands close against him*) Because I must go—my business is elsewhere—I ought never to have seen you or spoken to you—but I

had to come to this house—and you were here—
and how could I help it? Oh—I couldn't—for my
whole—it's only you in the—(*stops. Recovers. Releases her hands. Turns blindly* R.—*Then as if to
go* L.) Your mother—I'll say good-bye to her!

EDITH. (C. *on his* L. *Going quickly in his way*)
No!—You must listen! They need you here in
Richmond!—The President told me so himself!—
Your orders are to stay! You are given a Special
Commission on the War Department Telegraph ser-
vice, and you——

THORNE. (C. *Quickly, decisively, but in subdued
voice*) No! No! I won't take it! I couldn't take
it Miss Varney!

EDITH. You'll do that much for me!

THORNE. (*holding her hands*) It's for you that
I'll do nothing of the kind! If you ever think of me
again remember I refused it!

EDITH. (*breaking into* THORNE'S *last few words*)
You can't refuse! It's the President's request—it's
his order! (*leaving him and going toward door*)
Please wait a minute! I left it upstairs and you'll
see——

THORNE. No! Don't get it!—(*following her*)
Don't get it! I won't look at it!

EDITH. (*stops and turns*) But I want you to
see what it is! It puts you at the head of everything!
You have entire control! When you see it Ah know
you'll accept! Please wait! (EDITH *exits at door
up* L. *and runs up the stairway*)

THORNE. (*as she goes*) Miss Varney—I can't——
EDITH. (*as she goes*) Oh yes you can!

   (THORNE *stands looking off after* EDITH *for an
      instant. Then turns and hurries down to table
      L. C. and seizing his hat, starts rapidly up to-
      wards door up* L. *as if to go.—As* THORNE *starts
      down for hat sound of heavy door outside* L.
      opening and closing with a bang.)

(*Enter at door up* L. CAROLINE MITFORD, *skipping in lightly and quick after sound of door, crossing back of* THORNE *to up* C. *She is breathless from having run across the street.—Her dress is made of what is supposed to have been a great grandmother's wedding gown as light and pretty as possible—with a touch of the old-fashioned in cut and pattern. She is very young, girlish, lively and attractive. Has a slight assumption of military air in way of speaking and in her behavior, upon occasions when it comes in.*)

CAROLINE. (*comes quickly on to* C. *without seeing* THORNE. *Seeing* THORNE—*stops abruptly*) Oh!— Good evening!

THORNE. (*stepping aside to let her pass,— Mechanical salute with hat in right hand*) Miss Mitford! (*stands an instant in the doorway looking up the stairs, uncertain what to do*)

CAROLINE. (*saluting*) Yes of co'se—Ah forgot! —How lucky this is! You're just the very person Ah wanted to see! (*going toward lounge* R. C.) Ah'll tell you all about it in just a minute! Goodness me! (*sits*) Ah'm all out o'breath—just runnin' ovah from our house! (*sitting on the lounge* R. C. *and devoting herself to breathing for an instant*)

THORNE. (*going quickly down to* CAROLINE *at* R. C.) Miss Mitford—would you do something for me!

CAROLINE. Why of co'se Ah would!

THORNE. (*rapidly*) Thank you very much!—Tell Miss Varney when she comes down—Just say goodnight for me and tell her I've gone! (*turns* L. *quickly and starts toward door. Stops and turns to her when* CAROLINE *speaks*)

CAROLINE. (*pretending astonishment*) Why Ah wouldn't do such a thing for the wide, wide world! It would be a wicked dreadful lie—because you won't be gone!

THORNE. (*looking at* CAROLINE *from near* C. *for an instant. Then goes down near her*) I'm sorry you look at it that way.—Good-night, Miss Mitford! (*turns to go*)

CAROLINE. (*jumping to her feet and catching* THORNE *by right arm, going in front of him and coming round on his left between him and the door*) No no!—You don't seem to understand! Ah've got something to say to you!

THORNE. (*hurriedly*) Yes—but some other time —(*trying to go*)

CAROLINE. (*detaining him*) No no no!—Wait! (THORNE *stops*) There isn't any other time! It's to-night!—We're going to have a starvation party!

THORNE. Good heavens—another of those things!

CAROLINE. Yes—we are! It's goin' to be ovah at mah house this time! Now we'll expect you in half an hour. (*her finger up to emphasize the time*)

THORNE. Thank you, Miss Mitford, but I can't come! (*indicating off* L.) I've got to be—(*interrupted*)

CAROLINE. (*interrupting*) N—n—n—(*until she quiets him*) Now that wouldn't do at all! You went to Mamie Jones's! Would you treat me like that?

THORNE. Mamie Jones—that was last week Thursday—(CAROLINE *trying to stop him with* " now now—now! " *etc.*) Her mother—(CAROLINE *louder with her stammering* " now—now! " THORNE *raises his voice above the din*) Her mother——

(*As* CAROLINE *is still going on he gives it up and looks front in despair.*)

CAROLINE. (*when quiet has come.—Very distinctly*) Now there isn't any use o' talkin'!

THORNE. (*nod*) Yes I see that!

CAROLINE. Didn't you promise to obey when Ah gave orders? Well, these are orders! (*she turns* L.)

THORNE. (*turning to her for a last attempt*) Yes, but this time——

CAROLINE. (*turns on him*) This time is just the same as all the other times only worse! (*turns away and goes to back of table* L. C. *and picks up flower*) (THORNE *looks at her, then turns and goes a little way toward up* R. C. *as if discouraged*)

CAROLINE. (*without turning*) Besides that she expects it.

(THORNE *turns at once and looks across at* CAROLINE.)

THORNE. What did you say? (*he moves down* C. *toward her*)

CAROLINE. (*at table* L. C.—*Smelling a flower daintily. Facing front*) Ah say—she expects it—that's all!

THORNE. Who do you mean?

CAROLINE. (*turns and looks at him*) Who?

THORNE. (*assent*) Um hm!

CAROLINE. (*innocently*) Who expects you?

THORNE. (*assent again*) Ah ha!

CAROLINE. Why Edith of co'se! Who did you s'pose Ah was talkin' about all this time?

THORNE. Oh! She expects me to—(*gesture up toward door up* L.)

CAROLINE. Why of co'se she does!—Just to take her ovah!—Goodness me! You needn't stay if you don't want to! Now Ah'll go an' tell her you're waiting—that's what Ah'll do. (*starts up toward door up* L. C.—*Stops and turns at door*) You won't go now?

THORNE. If she expects it Miss Mitford (*moving up toward* CAROLINE) I'll wait an' take her over—but I can't stay a minute!

CAROLINE. Well Ah thought you'd come to your senses some time or other!—You don't seem to quite realize what you've got to do!—See here, Mr. Captain—(*bringing him down* c. *a little with her—on her right*) Was she most ready?

THORNE. (*hesitates*) Well—e—how do I—how—

CAROLINE. What dress did she have on?

THORNE. (*looks down at* CAROLINE *an instant before speaking*)—Dress?

CAROLINE. Oh, you men! Why she's only got two!

THORNE. (*relieved*) Yes—well then very likely this was one of them, Miss Mitford!

CAROLINE. (*letting go his arm. Starting up toward door*) Oh, no mattah—Ah'm going up anyway! (THORNE *moves up* c. *as* CAROLINE *goes up* L. C. CAROLINE *stops up* L. C. *near door and turns to* THORNE) Cap'n Thorne—you can wait out there on the veranda! (*pointing to window up* R.)

THORNE. (*glances where she points—then to her*) I know—but if I wait right here she'll——

CAROLINE. (*majestically*) Those are orders! (THORNE *looks at her an instant—then salutes and wheels about making complete turn to* R. *and starts toward the window at* R. CAROLINE *is watching him admiringly. As* THORNE *reaches* R. C.) It's cooler outside you know!

THORNE. (*turning to her at* R. C. *and standing in stiff military attitude*) Pardon me, Miss Mitford—orders never have to be explained!

CAROLINE. That's right!—I take back the explanation! (*with odd little salute stepping one step to her* R. *on it*)

THORNE. (*with deferential salute in slight imitation of hers—but with step to his left*) That's right Miss Mitford—take it back! (*Turns and is reaching to pull aside curtains of window with right hand*)

CAROLINE. And—oh yes!—Cap'n!

(THORNE *turns to her again questioningly—right hand still holding curtain behind him.*)

CAROLINE. (*a peremptory order*) Smoke!

(*For an instant* THORNE *does not understand. Then he sees it and relapses at once into easy manner, stepping forward a little and feeling with right hand in coat front for cigar—turning somewhat to front.*)

THORNE. (*as above—after seeing it*) Oh—ha ha—(*smiling*) you mean one of those Nashville sto—
CAROLINE. Silence sir! (THORNE *looks round at her quickly*) Orders never have to be explained!
THORNE. (*with salute*) Right again Miss Mitford—orders never have to be explained! (*Exits at window up* R.)
CAROLINE. (*looks admiringly after* THORNE) He's splendid! If Wilfred was only like that! (*thinks*) But then—our engagement's broken off anyway so what's the diff!—Only—if he was like that—Ah'd—no! Ah don't think Ah'd—(*shakes head*)

(*Enter* MRS. VARNEY *at door Left.* CAROLINE *does not notice her until she comes near—then breaks off in middle of sentence about* WILFRED *and goes right on in same breath.*)

Why how dy do!
MRS. VARNEY. Why Caroline dear! What are you talking about all to yourself!
CAROLINE. (*confused*) Oh—just—Ah was just saying you know—that—why Ah don't know—Ah don't really know what Ah was goin' to—e—Do you think it's goin' to rain?
MRS. VARNEY. Dear me, child—I haven't thought about it!—Why what have you got on?—Is that a new dress?
CAROLINE. New *dress*! Well Ah should think so! These are my great grandmother's mother's weddin' clothes! Aren't they just the most beau-

fleist you ever saw! Just in the nick of time too!
Ah was on my very last rags, an' Ah didn't know
what to do—an' Mama gave me a key and told me to
open an old horsehair trunk in the garret—an' Ah
did—and these were in it! (*takes a dance step or
two, holding it out*) Just in time for the starvation
party to-night! Ran ovah here to show it to Edith
—where is she?

Mrs. VARNEY. She won't be over to-night, I'm
afraid. (*crosses to* R. C.)

CAROLINE. (C.) Oh yes she will!

Mrs. VARNEY. But I've just come down dear!
Caroline. Yes—but Ah'm just going *up* dear!
(CAROLINE *turns and runs quickly up the stairs and
off to Left.* Mrs. VARNEY *alone a moment. After
a little she moves down front in thought. Then
turns to desk* R. *and prepares to write a letter. Suddenly* CAROLINE *races down the stairs again and runs
lightly on at door up* L. Mrs. VARNEY *looks up surprised.* CAROLINE *hurries across toward window up*
R. *as if going out*) You see Caroline, it was no use!

CAROLINE. (*turning*) No use! (*comes down in
front of couch near* Mrs. VARNEY)

Mrs. VARNEY (*at desk* R.) Why you don't mean
—in this short time——

CAROLINE. Goodness me! Ah didn't stop to
argue with her—Ah just told her!

Mrs. VARNEY. Told her what, child!

CAROLINE. Why—that Cap'n Thorne was waitin'
for her out yere on the v'randah!

Mrs. VARNEY. She isn't going is she?

CAROLINE. Well, Ah wouldn't like to say for sure
—(*moving nearer* Mrs. VARNEY *and lower voice*)
but you just watch which dress she has on when she
comes down! Now Ah'll go out there an' tell him
she'll be down in a minute—then the whole thing's
finished up all round! Ah have more trouble getting
people fixed so they can come to my party than it

would take to run a blockade into Savannah every
fifteen minutes! (*she runs off at window up* R. *going
around in front of couch to do*)

(MRS. VARNEY *looks after* CAROLINE *with a smile
for a moment, and then taking some paper and
envelopes in her hand, rises and moves as if to go
to door up* L. *Enter* WILFRED *at door up* L.
*coming in as if he wished to avoid being seen,
and looking off up stairway as he enters. He
carries a package under his coat, which is done
up in a paper loosely.* WILFRED *turns quickly
seeing* MRS. VARNEY *and makes a very slight
movement as if to conceal the package he carries.
He stands looking at her.*)

MRS. VARNEY. What have you got there Wilfred?
WILFRED. Here? (*brings out package*) O—it's
only—(*looks at her a little guiltily*) Have you
written that letter yet?
MRS. VARNEY. No dear—I've been too busy.
But I'm going to do it right now. (MRS. VARNEY
goes across to door at L. *Near the door she glances
round a little anxiously at* WILFRED. WILFRED *is
looking at her. Then she exits at door up* L. *and goes
up the stairs*)

(WILFRED *turns away after she has gone. Glances
round room.—Goes down to table* L. C. *and
begins to undo the package cautiously. He has
hardly got the paper loosened—just enough to
enable audience to see that it contains a pair of
military trousers, when* CAROLINE *appears at
window up* R.)

CAROLINE. (*speaking off at window* R.) Those are
orders Cap'n—an' orders never have to be explained!

(WILFRED *hurriedly stuffs the trousers inside his coat
and buttons it over them.*)

THORNE. (*outside up* R.—*at a little distance*) Perfectly right Miss Mitford!

(CAROLINE *enters through window up* R. *closing it after her, but does not close portieres.* WILFRED *is about to start toward down* L. CAROLINE *turning from window* R. *sees* WILFRED.)

CAROLINE. Good evening Mr. Varney.

WILFRED. (*coldly*) Good evening Miss Mitford! (*both now start rapidly toward door up* L. *but as it brings them toward each other they stop simultaneously up stage in order to avoid meeting*)

CAROLINE. Excuse me—Ah'm in a hurry!

WILFRED. That's plain enough! (*looks at her*) Another party Ah reckon!

CAROLINE. (C.) You reckon perfectly correct—it *is* another party!

WILFRED. (L. C.) Dancing!

CAROLINE. (*speaks emphatically*) What of it? What's the matter with dancing Ah'd like to know!

WILFRED. Nothing's the matter with it—if you want to *do* it!

CAROLINE. Well Ah want to *do* it fast enough if that's all you mean!

WILFRED. But I must say it's a pretty way to carry on—with the sound of the cannon not six miles away! (*goes down stage* L.)

(WILFRED *is dead in earnest not only in this scene but in all his scenes.*)

CAROLINE. (*turns and comes down a little* C. *after him*) What do you want us to do? Sit down and cry about it?—That would do a heap o' good now wouldn't it?

WILFRED. Oh—I haven't time to talk about it! (*starts to go*)

CAROLINE. Well it was you who started out to talk about it—Ah'm right sure Ah didn't!

WILFRED. (*up* L. C. *After glance to see that no one is near turns on her*) Oh—you needn't try to fool me! Ah know well enough how you've been carrying on since our engagement was broken off! Half a dozen officers proposing to you—a dozen for all Ah know!

CAROLINE. (*down* C. *a little*) What difference does it make? Ah haven't got to marry 'em have I?

WILFRED. (L. C.) Well—(*twist of head*) it isn't very nice to go on like that Ah must say—proposals by the wholesale! (*turning away*)

CAROLINE. (R. C.) Goodness gracious—what's the use of talking to me about it? *They're* the ones that propose—*Ah* don't!

WILFRED. (L. C. *turning on her*) Well what do you let 'em do it for?

CAROLINE. (R. C.) How can Ah help it?

WILFRED. (L. C.) Ho! (*sneer*) Any girl can help it! You helped it with me all right!

CAROLINE. (R. C.) Well—that was different! (*a queer look at him*)

WILFRED. (L. C.) And ever since you threw me ovah—

CAROLINE. (R. C. *indignantly*) Oh!—Ah *didn't* throw you ovah—you just *went* ovah! (*turns away to* R. *a little*)

WILFRED. (L. C.) Well—Ah went over because you walked off alone with Major Sillsby that night we were at Drury's Bluff an' encouraged him to propose—(CAROLINE *looks round in wrath*) Yes—encouraged him!

CAROLINE. (R. C.) Of co'se Ah did! Ah didn't want 'im hangin' round forever did Ah? That's the on'y way to finish 'em off!

WILFRED. (L. C.) You want to finish too many of 'em off! Nearly every officer in the 17th Virginyah Ah'll be sworn!

CAROLINE. (R. C.) What do you want me to do—

string a placard round my neck saying "No proposals received here—apply at the office!" Would that make you feel any better?

WILFRED. (L. C.) (*throwing it off with pretended carelessness*) Oh—it doesn't make any difference to me what you do!

CAROLINE. Well if it doesn't make any difference to you, it doesn't even make as much as that to me! (*turns and sits on end of couch* R. C.)

WILFRED. (*turning on her again and going toward her to down* C.) Oh—it doesn't! Ah think it does though!—You looked as if you enjoyed it pretty well while the 3rd Virginyah was in the city!

CAROLINE. Enjoyed it! Ah should think Ah did! (*jumping up*) Ah just love every one of 'em!— They're on their way to the front! They're going to fight for us—an' an' die for us—an' Ah love 'em (*turns away*)

WILFRED. (C.) Well why don't you accept one of 'em an' done with it!

CAROLINE. (R. C. *turning on him*) How do you know but what Ah'm going to?

WILFRED. (*goes toward her a little*) Ah suppose it'll be one of those smart young fellows with a cavalry uniform!

CAROLINE. (R. C.) It'll be *some* kind of a uniform! It won't be anyone that stays in Richmond— Ah can tell you that!

WILFRED. (*a little* R. *of* C.) (*after looking at her —unable for a moment to speak—Looks round room helplessly*) (*low voice*) Now I see what it was! I had to stay in Richmond—an' so you—(*unable to go on*)

CAROLINE. (*in front of couch* R. C.) Well—(*Looking down—playing with something with her foot*) that made a heap o' difference! (*looks up.—Different tone*) Why Ah was the on'y girl on Franklin Street that didn't have a—a—(*hesitates*)—someone she was engaged to at the front! The on'y one! Just think what it was—to be out of it like that! (WILFRED *simply looks at her*) Why you've no idea what Ah suffered! Besides, it's our—our *duty* to help all we can!

WILFRED. (*near her on her* L.) (*hoarsely*) Help! (*thinking of his trousers*)

CAROLINE. Yes—help! There aren't many things we girls can do—Ah know that well enough! But Colonel Woodbridge—he's one o' Morgan's men you know—well he told Mollie Pickens that the boys fight *twice* as well when they have a—a sweetheart at home! (WILFRED *glances about quickly*)

· WILFRED. (*after glance about*) He said that did he?

CAROLINE. Yes—an' if we can make 'em fight twice as well—why we just ought to do it—that's all! We girls can't do much but we can do something!

WILFRED. (*short pause.—He makes an absent-minded motion of feeling of the package under his arm*) You're in earnest are you?

CAROLINE. Earnest!

WILFRED. You really want to help—all you can!

CAROLINE. Well Ah should think so!

WILFRED. An' if Ah was—(*glances around cautiously*) If I was going to join the army would you help me?

CAROLINE. (*looking front and down. Slight embarrassment*) Why of co'se Ah would—if it was anything Ah could do!

WILFRED. (*earnestly—quite near her*) Oh it's something you can do all right—Ah'm sure o' that!

CAROLINE. (R. C. *Hardly daring to look up*) What is it?

WILFRED. (C. *Unrolling a pair of old gray army trousers taking them from under his coat so that they spread before her on cue*) Cut these off! (*Short pause.* CAROLINE *looking at trousers.* WILFEFRD

looking at her. WILFRED *soon goes on very earnestly,
holding them before his own legs to measure)*
They're about twice too long! All you got to do is
to cut 'em off about there—an' sew up the ends so
they won't ravel out!

CAROLINE. (R. C. *The idea beginning to dawn on
her*) Why they're for the Army! (*taking trousers
and hugging them to her—legs hanging down)*

WILFFRED. (C.) Sh!—Don't speak so loud for
heaven's sake! (*a glance back as if afraid of being
overheard*) Ah've got a jacket here too! (*shows
her a small army coat*) Nearly a fit—came from
the hospital—Johnny Seldon wore it—he won't want
it any more you know——an' he was just about my
size!

CAROLINE. (R. C. *Low voice*) No—he won't
want it any more. (*stands thinking*)

WILFRED. (C. *After a slight pause*) Well!—Ah
thought you said you wanted to help!

CAROLINE. (R. C. *Quickly*) Oh yes—Ah do! Ah
do!

WILFRED. (C.) Well go on—what are you waiting
for?

CAROLINE. (R. C. *near end of couch*) Yes! Yes!
(*hurriedly drops on knees on floor and takes hold
spreading trousers out exactly and patting them
smooth*) This is the place isn't it? (*pointing to
near the knees*)

WILFRED. No—not up there—Here! (*indicating
about 3 inches from the bottom of the trouser leg*)

CAROLINE. Oh yes! Ah see! (*hurriedly snatches
pins from her dress. Puts one in mouth and one in
place* WILFRED *indicates.—All very rapid and earnest.
—Takes hold of other leg of trousers)*

(NOTE: *Only motions of putting pins in mouth—
do not actually use pins. Stage Manager see to
this without fail.*)

(*Speaking as if pin in mouth. Innocently—and without looking up*) The other one just the same? (*a musical rise to voice at end of this.* WILFRED *does not deign to reply.* CAROLINE *hearing nothing looks up at him*) Oh yes, o' co'se! (*she quickly puts pin in other leg of trousers*)

(NOTE: *From trouser business* CAROLINE'S *demeanor toward* WILFRED *is entirely changed. It is because he is going to join the Army.*)

(CAROLINE *on floor with trousers and coat takes hold of the work with enthusiasm—very busy—pins—etc. —etc.*) Do you see any scissors around anywhere! (WILFRED *dashes about looking on tables, after putting jacket on end of couch* R. C.) This won't never tear—(*trying to tear off the trousers' leg*)— for all Ah can do!

WILFRED. (*first looking on table down* L. C. *and picking up paper jacket was wrapped in. Getting a work-basket from table up* C. *and quickly bringing it*) There must be some in here! (*hands the scissors out of the basket to* CAROLINE.—*As she reaches up from her position on the floor to take them, she looks in* WILFRED'S *face an instant—then quickly down to work again. Then she works with head down.* WILFRED *leaves wrapping paper up stage out of the way*)

(*Slight pause.*)

CAROLINE. (*on her knees* R. C. *near couch. Low voice—not looking up at him*) When are you goin' to wear 'em?

WILFRED. (C.) When they're cut off!

(CAROLINE *looks up at him. Thread or scissors in mouth.*)

CAROLINE. You mean—you're really——
WILFRED. Um hm! (*assent*)
CAROLINE. But your mother——

WILFRED.   She knows it.

CAROLINE.   Oh!

WILFRED.   She's going to write the General to-night.

CAROLINE.   But how about if he won't let you?

WILFRED.   (*with boyish determination—but keeping voice down*) Ah'll go just the same!

CAROLINE.   (*suddenly jumps to her feet dropping everything on the floor and catches his hand*) Oh Ah'm *so* glad! Why it makes another thing of it! When Ah said that about staying in Richmond Ah didn't know! Oh, Ah do want to help all I can!

WILFRED.   (*who has been regarding her burst of enthusiasm rather coldly*) You do!

CAROLINE.   Indeed—indeed Ah do!

WILFRED.   Then cut those off for Heaven's sake!

CAROLINE.   Oh yes! (*she catches up trousers. jacket, etc., and sits quickly on lounge and excitedly paws them over*). Where shall Ah cut 'em?

WILFRED.   The same place—Ah haven't grown any!

CAROLINE.   Dear me—Ah don't know where it was!

WILFRED.   You stuck some pins in!

CAROLINE.   (*finding pins*) Oh yes—here they are! (*seizing the trousers and going to work soon cutting off one of the trousers' legs*)

WILFRED.   That's it!

CAROLINE.   When did you say she was going to write.

WILFRED.   To-night.

CAROLINE.   (*looking up with distrust*) She doesn't want you to go does she?

WILFRED.   Ah don't reckon she does—very much!

CAROLINE.   She'll tell him not to let you!

WILFRED.   (*looks at her with wide open eyes*) No!

CAROLINE.   That's the way they always do!

WILFRED.   The devil!

CAROLINE. Ah should think so!

WILFRED. What can Ah do!

CAROLINE. Write to him yourself.

WILFRED. Good idea!

CAROLINE. Then you can just tell him what you like!

WILFRED. Ah'll tell him Ah *can't* stay here!

CAROLINE. (*excitedly rising—letting the jacket fall on floor at one side*) Tell him you're coming anyhow!

WILFRED. Ah will!

CAROLINE. Whether he says so or not!

WILFRED. Then he'll say so won't he?

CAROLINE. O' co'se he will—there ain't anything else to say!

WILFRED. Ah'll do it! (*starts to go up* L. *Stops and goes back to* CAROLINE) Say—you're pretty good! (*catching one of* CAROLINE's *hands impulsively.* CAROLINE *looks down at work in her hand*) Ah'll go upstairs an' write it now! (*starts toward door up* L. CAROLINE *watches him.—He turns back and she looks quickly down at her work again*) Finish those things as soon as you can an' leave 'em here—in the hall closet! (*indicating outside* L.)

CAROLINE. (*nodding her head*) Yes!

WILFRED. An' don't let anyone see 'em whatever you do!

CAROLINE. (*shaking her head*) No!

(WILFRED *hurries off at door up* L. CAROLINE *looks after him with expression of ecstasy—lapsing into dreaminess as she turns to front. Suddenly bethinks herself with a start and a little " O " and slipping down on floor near chair she goes excitedly to work on the trousers cutting at the other leg with violence and rapidly, getting it nearly cut through so that later it dangles by a few threads. Suddenly she stops work and listens. Then with great haste she gathers up all the things she can, leaving the jacket however where it fell, and jumps to her feet with them in her arms, hugging the confused bundle close against her and hastily tucking in portions that hang out so that* MRS. VARNEY *won't see what it is.)*

(Enter MRS. VARNEY *up* L. *coming down the stairway and into the room.)*

MRS. VARNEY. Oh—you haven't gone yet!

CAROLINE. Not quite!—I mean not yet!—It doesn't begin for an hour you know!

MRS. VARNEY. What doesn't begin?

CAROLINE. The party!

MRS. VARNEY. Oh—then you have plenty of time! *(turning as if to go up* C.)

CAROLINE. *(hastening across toward door* L. *with her arms full of things)* Yes—but Ah'll have to go now sure enough! *(near* C. *she drops the scissors)*

MRS. VARNEY. *(up* C. *Turning)* You dropped your scissors dear!

CAROLINE. Oh! *(coming back for them)* I—I thought I heard something! *(in picking them up she lets the cut-off end of a trouser leg fall but does not notice it and goes toward door up* L.)

MRS. VARNEY. *(coming down* C.) What are you making, Caroline?

CAROLINE. *(turning near door up* L.) Oh—Ah was just altering a dress—that's all! *(turning to go)*

MRS. VARNEY. *(stooping and picking up the piece of trouser leg)* Here, Carrie!—you dropped a—a— *(looks at it)*

CAROLINE. *(hurrying to* MRS. VARNEY *and snatching the piece—stuffing it in with rest)* Oh yes!— *(looks at* MRS. VARNEY *an instant. The other piece of the trouser leg is hanging by its shred in full sight*) That—that was one of the sleeves! (*turns and hurries off at door up* L. *and exits door* R. *below stairway*)

(MRS. VARNEY *after a moment turns and goes toward door up* C. *Seeing something on the couch* R. C. *she stops and goes to pick it up. On coming to it she finds the little gray soldier's jacket left by* CAROLINE *in her hasty scramble.* MRS. VARNEY *stoops and picks it up and stands looking at it facing front.*)

(*After a brief pause the loud sound of hurried opening of front door outside left and tramp of heavy feet on the floor is heard.*)

(MRS. VARNEY *looks up and across left, letting the coat fall on end of couch* R. C.)

(*Enter* MR. BENTON ARRELSFORD—*up* L. *from* L.—*a tall fine looking Southern man of about 35 or 40 dressed in citizen's clothes—black Prince Albert coat, etc.—Rather distinguished appearance. He is seen outside door up* L. *hurriedly placing a guard of Confederate soldiers at doors outside up left, also at foot of stairs, and at any other exit in sight.* MRS. VARNEY *much surprised, moves toward door* L. MR. ARRELSFORD *at the same time and as noiselessly as possible, hastens into the room.*)

MRS. VARNEY. (*as he enters*) Mr. Arrelsford! (*goes toward* C. *up a little*)

ARRELSFORD. (*comes quickly across to* MRS. VARNEY. *Speaks in a low voice and rapidly*) Ah was obliged to come in without ceremony, Mrs. Varney. You'll understand when I tell you what it is!

MRS. VARNEY. And those men—(*motions toward the men outside door up* C. L. C.)

ARRELSFORD. (*low voice*) They're on guard at the doors out there!

Mrs. Varney. (*low voice*) On guard!—You mean——

Arrelsford. Ah'm very much afraid we've got to put you to a little inconvenience, Mrs. Varney! (*glances about cautiously.* Mrs. Varney *stands astonished*) Is there anybody in that room? (*pointing to door up* c.)

Mrs. Varney. Yes—a number of ladies sewing for the hospitals.

Arrelsford. Kindly come this way a little. (*going down* l. c. *with* Mrs. Varney) One of your servants has got himself into trouble, Mrs. Varney, an' we're compelled to have him watched!

Mrs. Varney. What kind of trouble?

Arrelsford. (*low voice*) Pretty serious ma'am! That's the way it looks now!—You've got an old white-haired niggah here——

Mrs. Varney. You mean Jonas?

Arrelsford. Ah believe that's his name!

Mrs. Varney. You suspect him of something!

Arrelsford. (*keeping voice down*) We don't suspect—we *know* what he's done! (*glances round before going on*) He's been down in the Libby Prison under pretense of selling something to the Yankees we've got in there, an' he now has on his person a written communication from one of them which he intends to deliver to some Yankee agent here in Richmond! (Arrelsford *goes around in front of table and up* l. *of it to near door up* l. c.)

(Mrs. Varney *motionless a second looking at* Arrelsford. *She soon recovers.*)

Mrs. Varney. Send for the man! (*starting to move up stage and toward* l.) Let us see if this—

Arrelsford. (*up* l. c. *near* r. *upper corner of table* l. c. *Quickly stopping her*) No! Not yet! (*Glances quickly round at doors and windows—then speaks in lowered voice but with great intensity and clearness*) Ah've got to get that paper! If he's alarmed he'll destroy it! Ah've got to have it! It'll give us the clue to one o' their cursed plots! They've been right close on this town for months—trying to break down our defenses and get in on us. This is some rascally game they're at to weaken us from the inside! Two weeks ago we got word from our agents that we keep over there in the Yankee lines telling us that two brothers—Lewis and Henry Dumont— have been under Secret Service orders to do some rascally piece of work here in Richmond. We had close descriptions of these fellows but we've never been able to lay our hands on 'em till last night!

MRS. VARNEY. (*up* C. *and a little* L. *near* ARRELS-FORD. *Intense whisper*) You've got them?

ARRELSFORD. (*up* L. C. *Low voice, but intense*) We've got one o' them! An' it won't take long to run down the othah!

MRS. VARNEY. (*low voice, great intensity*) The one—the one you caught—was he here in Richmond?

ARRELSFORD. (*low voice*) No—he was brought in last night with a lot o' men we captured making a raid.

MRS. VARNEY. Taken prisoner!

ARRELSFORD. (*nods affirmatively, glances round*) Let himself be taken! That's one of their tricks for getting through our lines when they want to bring a message or give some signal.

MRS. VARNEY. You mean, they get into Libby Prison?

ARRELSFORD. (*low voice. Great intensity*) Yes! Damn them! (*this oath indistinctly between his teeth*) But we were on the lookout for this man and we spotted him pretty quick. I gave orders not to search him or to take away his clothes but to put him in with the others and keep the closest watch on him that was ever kept on a man! We knew from his coming in that his brother must be here in the city and he'd send a message to him the first chance he got.

MRS. VARNEY. (*low voice*)   But Jonas!—How could he——

ARRELSFORD. (*low and intense*)   Easy enough! He comes down to Libby to sell goubers to the prisoners—we let 'im pass in—he fools around awhile until he gets a chance to brush against this man Dumont—we're watching an' we see a bit of paper pass between 'em! The old rascal's got that paper now ma'am, an' besides these men in heah I've got a dozen more on the outside watching him through the windows! (*turns and moves up glancing off up* L. *with some anxiety*)

MRS. VARNEY. (*after slight pause. Turns. Speaks in intense but subdued voice. Almost whisper*)   The man he gives it to!   *He's* the one you want!

ARRELSFORD. (*approaching her quickly, low voice but intense*)   Yes! But I can't wait long! If the niggah sees a man or hears a sound he'll destroy it before we can jump in on 'im—an' I must have that paper! (*strides quickly up,* MRS. VARNEY *following a step or two. Speaking off up* L. *in low but sharp voice*)   Corporal!

(*Enter* CORPORAL *at door up* L. *from* L. *he salutes and stands.*)

How is it now?

CORPORAL. (*low voice*)   All quiet sir!

(ARRELSFORD *and* MRS. VARNEY *face each other.*)

ARRELSFORD. (*low, intense*)   It won't do to wait— I've got to get that paper! It's the key to the game they're trying to play against us!

MRS. VARNEY. (*intense. Half whisper*)   No no! The man he's going to give it to!   Get him!

ARRELSFORD. (*low—intense*)   That paper might give us a clue! If not I'll make the niggah tell!

Damn it—I'll shoot it out of him! (*turns to* CORPORAL) How quick can you get at him from that door! (*pointing off up* L.)

CORPORAL. (*no salute, low voice*) It's through a hallway—and across the dining-room.

ARRELSFORD. (*low voice*) Well, take two men and——

MRS. VARNEY. (*interrupting—touching* ARRELSFORD *to stop him. Low voice*) Why not keep your men out of sight and let me send for him—here?

ARRELSFORD. (*after a second's thought. Low voice*) That's better! We'll get 'im in here! While you're talking to him they can nab him from behind! (*turns to* CORPORAL) You heard!

CORPORAL. (*low voice*) Yes, sir.

ARRELSFORD. (*low voice*) Keep your men out of sight—get 'em back there in the hall—an' while we're making him talk send a man down each side and pin him! Hold 'im stiff! He mustn't destroy any paper he's got!

(CORPORAL *salutes and exits with men up* L. *and off* L. MRS. VARNEY *turns to* ARRELSFORD *who is well up* C. *with her hand on the bell rope.*)

MRS. VARNEY. (*low voice*) Now, Mr. Arrelsford?

ARRELSFORD. Yes.

(MRS. VARNEY *rings the bell. Short pause. Enter* MARTHA *at door up* L. *She stands in the doorway.*)

MRS. VARNEY. (*down* L. *near mantel*) Is there anyone I can send to the hospital, Martha?

MARTHA. (*up* L. C. *in doorway*) Luther's out yere, mam.

MRS. VARNEY. Luther? (*considers*) No—he's too small. I don't want a boy.

MARTHA. Jonas is yere, mam—if you want him.

MRS. VARNEY. Oh, Jonas—yes! Tell 'im to come in here right away.

MARTHA. Yaas'm. (*exits at door up* L.)

(MRS. VARNEY *crosses back of table* L. C. *goes toward* R. C. *and sits on couch.* ARRELSFORD *waits up* C.)

(OLD JONAS *appears at the door up* L. *coming from door* R. *below stairs. He is a thick-set gray-haired old negro. He comes a few steps into the room.*)

(MRS. VARNEY *looks at* JONAS *and he at her.—At first he is entirely unsuspecting, but in a moment, seeing* ARRELSFORD *standing up* C. *his eyes shift about restlessly for an instant.*)

MRS. VARNEY. (*on couch* R. C.) Jonas——
JONAS. (*up* L. C.) Yes mam.
MRS. VARNEY. Have you any idea why I sent for you?
JONAS. Ah heers you was wantin' to sen' to de hossiple ma'am.

(CORPORAL *and* MEN *enters* L. *to behind* JONAS.)
MRS. VARNEY. Oh—then Martha told you.

(CORPORAL *motions to* MEN *and they instantly step forward—one on each side of* JONAS, *and stand motionless.*)

JONAS. Waal she didn't ezzackly say whut you— (*sees man each side of him and stops in the midst of his speech. He does not start, but is frozen with terror. Stands motionless. Expression of face scarcely changes. Soon he lowers his eyes and then begins stealthily to get his right hand toward his inside breast pocket*)

(CORPORAL *gives a sharp order. The* MEN *instantly seize* JONAS. CORPORAL *quickly feels in his pocket.* JONAS *struggles desperately but in an instant the* CORPORAL *has the paper which he hands—with a salute—to* ARRELSFORD—*coming*

forward in front of MEN *and* JONAS *to do so—
then goes back to* L. *of* MEN *and* JONAS.)

(MRS. VARNEY *rises as men seize* JONAS.)

ARRELSFORD. (*down* R. *of* MEN *and* JONAS)   See if
there's anything more!   (ARRELSFORD *goes up back of
men to lamp*)

(CORPORAL *quickly searches* JONAS.   MEN *still holding him, raising his arms above his head, etc.
After the search* MEN *release* JONAS *and stand
guard one on each side of him.*)

CORPORAL. (*on salute*)   That's all sir.

(ARRELSFORD *turns to lamp on table up* C. *opening
the paper as he does so, while* CORPORAL *is
searching* JONAS.   MRS. VARNEY *watches him
intently.   ARRELSFORD *reads the paper quickly
and at once wheels round on* JONAS *coming down
R. of him and* MEN.)

ARRELSFORD. (*low voice—but sharp and telling*)
Who was this for?   (JONAS *stands silent*)   If you
don't tell it's going to be mighty bad for you!—
(JONAS *stands silent looking at* ARRELSFORD.   *After
pause* ARRELSFORD *turns to* MRS. VARNEY)   I'm
right sorry ma'am, but it looks like we've got to shoot
'im!   (*eyeing* JONAS.   *Goes down* C.)   Corporal!
(*Motions* CORPORAL *to approach.—*CORPORAL *steps
to* ARRELSFORD *on salute.   To* CORPORAL.—*Low
voice*)   Take him outside and get it out of him!
String him up till he talks!   You understand!
(CORPORAL *salutes and is about to turn*)   Here!
(CORPORAL *turns back to* ARRELSFORD *on salute.
ARRELSFORD *glances toward the window at* R. *and
back* L.)   Go down on that side—back of the house!
(*pointing up* L.)   And keep it quiet!   Nobody must
know of this!   Not a soul!

(CORPORAL *salutes again.—Goes up to* MEN.—*Gives*

an order. MEN *turn on order and march* JONAS
off at door up L. *and off* L. *All very quick with
military precision. The* CORPORAL *goes with
them.* ARRELSFORD *stands watching exit of*
JONAS *and* MEN *until they are gone and the
sound of the closing of heavy front door is heard
outside left. He then turns to* MRS. VARNEY.
ARRELSFORD *and* MRS. VARNEY *keep voices down
to nearly a whisper in the coming scene—but
with utmost force and intensity.*)

MRS. VARNEY. (*indicating the paper in his
hand*) Was there anything in that——
ARRELSFORD. (*near* MRS. VARNEY *on her* L.)
We've got the trick they want to play!
MRS. VARNEY. But not the man—not the man
who is to play it!
ARRELSFORD. I didn't say that!
MRS. VARNEY. There's a clue?
ARRELSFORD. There *is* a clue!
MRS. VARNEY. Will it answer? Do you know
who——
ARRELSFORD. (*interrupting*) As plain as if we
had his name!
MRS. VARNEY. Thank God! (*motionless an
instant. Then she extends her hand for the paper*)
Let me see! (ARRELSFORD *momentary hesitation—
then hands her the paper. She looks at paper, then
reads it aloud*) "ATTACK TO-NIGHT—PLAN
3—USE TELEGRAPH"—(*slight motion or sound
from* ARRELSFORD *to quiet her and a quick glance
round. Low voice—half whisper*) What does it
mean?
ARRELSFORD. (*takes paper. Low voice but
incisive*) They attack to-night!—The place where
they strike is indicated by "Plan 3." (*finger on the
words on paper in his hand*)
MRS. VARNEY. Plan three?

ARRELSFORD. He knows what they mean by that!
—It's arranged beforehand!

MRS. VARNEY. And—the last—the last there!
(*quick look at the paper in* ARRELSFORD'S *hands*)
"Use Telegraph?"

ARRELSFORD. He's to use our War Department
Telegraph Lines to send some false order and weaken
that position—the one they indicate by "Plan
Three"—so they can break through and come down
on the city!

MRS. VARNEY. Oh! (*a breathless exclamation of
indignation. A second's pause—then suddenly*)
But the one—the man who is to do this—there's
nothing about *him!*

ARRELSFORD. There *is* something about him!

MRS. VARNEY. (*rapidly—almost run together*)
What? Where? I don't see it!

ARRELSFORD. "Use Telegraph!" (*the two
stand looking at one another*) We know every man
on the Telegraph Service—and every man of them's
true! But there's some who want to get into that
service that we don't know quite so well!

MRS. VARNEY. He would be one!

ARRELSFORD. There aren't so very many! (*these
speeches given suggestively—with slight pause after
each. All very low voice and intense*) It isn't every
man that's an expert!—The niggah brought this
paper to your house, Mrs. Varney?

MRS. VARNEY. My—(*hesitates—beginning to
realize*)

ARRELSFORD. (*wait for above hesitation by* MRS.
VARNEY) For more than a month your daughter
has been working to get an appointment for someone
on the Telegraph Service—perhaps *she* could give us
some idea——

(*A moment's pause—the two looking at one another.
Suddenly* MRS. VARNEY *turns and hurries to*

window up R. *and quickly pulls curtains together,*
turning and facing back to ARRELSFORD *at same*
instant.)

ARRELSFORD. (*almost whisper—but with utmost*
intensity) IS HE THERE? (MRS. VARNEY *nods*
affirmatively. She comes down toward ARRELSFORD)
Could he hear what we said?

MRS. VARNEY. (*shakes head negatively. Almost*
whisper) He's at the further end! (*comes back to*
R. *of* ARRELSFORD. ARRELSFORD *glances at windows*
R. *nervously.* MRS. VARNEY—*after a pause—low*
voice) You have a description you say!

ARRELSFORD. Yes—at the office.

MRS. VARNEY. Then this man—this Captain
Thorne—(*interrupted*)

ARRELSFORD. (*low voice—but with vehemence*)
There *is* no Captain Thorne! This fellow you have
in your house is Lewis Dumont! (*short pause*)

MRS. VARNEY. You mean—he came here to—
(*interrupted*)

ARRELSFORD. (*with vindictive fury breaking*
through in spite of himself—yet voice subdued almost
to a sharp whisper) He came to this town—he came
to this house—knowing your position and the in-
fluence of your name—for the sole purpose of getting
some hold on our Department Telegraph Line!
He's corrupted your servants—he's thick with the
men in the telegraph office—what he hasn't done
God A'mighty knows! But Washington ain't the
only place where there's a Secret Service! We've
got one here in Richmond! Oh—(*a shake of his*
head) two can play at that game—an it's my move
now! (*Goes up* R. C. *a few steps*)

(*Enter* EDITH VARNEY *running rapidly down stair-*
way up left and calling out excitedly as she
comes. She wears a white dress and has in her
hand the large official envelope which she took

upstairs in an earlier scene. ARRELSFORD *goes toward windows up* R.)

EDITH. (*as she runs down the stairway*) Mama! Mama!—Quick Mama! (MRS. VARNEY *hurries toward door up* L. *to meet her.* ARRELSFORD *turns in surprise looking toward door up* L. EDITH *meeting* MRS. VARNEY) Under my window—in the bushes—they're hurting someone frightfully!—Ah'm sure they are! Oh—come! (*starting toward door to lead the way.* MRS. VARNEY *stands looking at* EDITH. EDITH *stops surprised that* MRS. VARNEY *does not follow*) If you aren't coming Ah'll go myself! (*turning to go*)

MRS. VARNEY. Wait, Edith! (EDITH *stops up* L. C. *and turns back to* MRS. VARNEY) I must tell you something—it'll be a terrible shock I'm afraid! (EDITH *goes toward* MRS. VARNEY. ARRELSFORD *turns away a little—standing near* R. C. *watching window*) A man we trusted as a friend has shown himself a treacherous conspirator against us!

EDITH. (*up* L. C. *After a slight pause—low voice*) Who? (*pause.* MRS. VARNEY *up* C. *cannot bring herself to speak the name. After a slight pause —in the same low voice*) Who is it?

ARRELSFORD. (*down* R. C. *a little. Swinging round on her. Low voice but with vindictiveness*) It is the gentleman, Miss Varney, whose attentions you have been pleased to accept in the place of mine!

(*Short pause.* EDITH *looking at* ARRELSFORD, *white and motionless. Then she turns her face appealing to her mother.*—MRS. VARNEY *nods slowly in affirmation.* EDITH *puts the envelope with Commission in belt or bosom of dress in an absent manner.*)

EDITH. (*low voice*) Is it Mr. Arrelsford who makes this accusation?

ARRELSFORD. (*breaking out hotly but keeping voice down*) Yes—since you wish to know! From the first I've had my suspicions that this—(*he stops on seeing* EDITH'S *move toward the window up* R.)

(EDITH *turns on cue "Since you wish to know" and goes quickly toward the window up* R. *crossing* MRS. VARNEY. ARRELSFORD *breaks off in his speech and steps before her.*)

ARRELSFORD. (R. C. *low voice—speaking rapidly*) Where are you going?

EDITH. (C. *low voice*) For Captain Thorne.

ARRELSFORD. (*low voice*) Not now!

EDITH. (*turning with flashing indignation on* ARRELSFORD. *Low voice*) Mr. Arrelsford if this is something you're afraid to say to him—don't you *dare* say it to me!

ARRELSFORD. (*indignantly. Low voice*) Miss Varney, if you——

MRS. VARNEY. (L. C. *Interrupting quickly, low voice*) Edith, he has good reasons for not meeting Captain Thorne now!

EDITH. (*turning quickly to* MRS. VARNEY) Ah should think he had! The man who said that to his face wouldn't live to speak again!

MRS. VARNEY. My dear, you don't——

EDITH. (C.) Mama—this man has left his desk in the War Department so that he can have the pleasure of persecuting me! He's never attempted anything in the active service before! And when I ask him to face the man he accuses he turns like a coward!

ARRELSFORD. (*angrily, but keeping voice subdued*) Mrs. Varney, if she thinks—(*interrupted*)

EDITH. (*low voice*) I think nothing! I know a man of Captain Thorne's character is above suspicion!

ARRELSFORD. (*low voice*) His character! Ha ha! (*a sneer*) Where did he come from?—Who is he?

EDITH. (*low voice*)　Who are you?

ARRELSFORD.　That's not the question!

EDITH. (*low voice*)　Neither is it the question who is he! If it were I'd answer it—I'd tell you he's a soldier who has fought and been wounded for his country!

ARRELSFORD. (*low voice but incisive*)　We're not so sure of that!

EDITH. (*after a pause of indignation*)　He brought us letters from General Stonewall Jackson and—(*interrupted*)'

ARRELSFORD. (*quick and sharp*)　General Jackson was killed before his letter was presented!

EDITH.　What does·that signify, if he wrote it?

ARRELSFORD.　Nothing—*if* he wrote it!　(*accent strong on ' if '*)

EDITH.　Mr. Arrelsford, if you mean—(MRS. VARNEY *goes to* EDITH *putting her hand on* EDITH'S *arm*)

MRS. VARNEY. (*low voice*)　Listen Edith! They have proofs of a conspiracy on our Government Telegraph Lines. (ARRELSFORD *says " Sh " and goes to window up* R.　EDITH *turns from* ARRELSFORD *and looks before her listening on mention of " Telegraph Lines."* MRS. VARNEY *leads* EDITH *a little* L. *of* C. ARRELSFORD *stands near window up* R.)　Two men in the Northern Secret Service have been sent here to do this work. One is in Libby Prison. Our old Jonas went there to-day—secretly took a message from him and brought it here—to the other! (EDITH *turns toward* MRS. VARNEY *sharply*)　We've just had Jonas in here and found that paper on him!

(ARRELSFORD *comes down* R. *looking off through curtains at windows down* R.)

EDITH. (*rapidly, desperately. In low voice*)　But he hasn't said it was for——

(*Dull heavy sound of front door closing outside up* L.)

ARRELSFORD. (*low voice but incisively*) Not yet—but he will! (EDITH *looks at* ARRELSFORD *not comprehending. Enter* CORPORAL *at door up* L. *stands on salute.* LADIES *turn to him.* EDITH *breathless with anxiety.* MRS. VARNEY *calm but intent.* ARRELSFORD *goes across from* R. *to* CORPORAL *up* L. C. *Low voice*) Well—what does he say?

CORPORAL. (*low voice*) Nothing sir—he won't speak!

ARRELSFORD. (*sharply, but voice subdued*) What have you done?

CORPORAL. Strung him up three times and——

ARRELSFORD. (*enraged but keeping his voice down*) Well string him up again! If he won't speak shoot it out of him! Kill the dog! (*comes blindly down* L. CORPORAL *salutes and exits at door up* L. ARRELSFORD *turns to ladies and goes down* L. *back of table—gets hat from table*) We don't need the niggah's evidence—there's enough without it!

EDITH. (*up* C. *Low voice*) There's nothing!

ARRELSFORD. (L. *of table* L. C. *Low voice*) By twelve o'clock to-night you'll have all the proof you want!

EDITH. (*low voice*) There's no proof at all!

ARRELSFORD. (*low voice*) I'll show it to you at the telegraph office! Do you dare go with me?

EDITH. (*low voice*) Dare! (*moves toward him*) I *will* go with you!

ARRELSFORD. (*low voice*) I'll call for you in half an hour! (*goes up toward door up* L.)

EDITH. Wait!—what are you going to do?

ARRELSFORD. (*comes down back of table. Low voice but incisive*) I'm going to let him get this paper! He'll know what they want him to do—and then we'll see him try to do it!

EDITH. (L. C.) You're going to spy on him—hound him like a criminal!

ARRELSFORD. I'm going to prove what he is!

EDITH. (R. *of table* L. C. *Low voice*) Then prove it openly! Prove it at once! It's a shame to let a suspicion like that rest on an honorable man! Let him come in here and—(*interrupted*)

ARRELSFORD. (*low voice*) Impossible! (*goes down* L. *of table a little*)

EDITH. (*low voice*) Then do something else but do it now! (*turning away goes up* C. *a little, speaks desperately*) We must know that he is—that he's innocent! We must know that! (*a thought. Turns to* ARRELSFORD) You say the prisoner in Libby is his brother—that's what you said—his brother! Bring him here! Go to the prison and bring that man here!

ARRELSFORD. (L. *of table speaking across it. Subdued exclamation*) What!

EDITH. Let them meet! Bring them face to face! Then you can see whether——

ARRELSFORD. (*low voice, speaks rapidly*) You mean—bring them together here?

EDITH. Yes!

ARRELSFORD. As if the prisoner was trying to escape?

EDITH. Any way you like—but end it!

ARRELSFORD. When?

EDITH. Now!

ARRELSFORD. (*after instant's thought*) I'm willing to try that!—Can you keep him here? (*with a motion toward windows* R.)

EDITH. (*scarcely more than a movement of lips*) Yes.

ARRELSFORD. It won't be more than half an hour. Be out there on the veranda. When I tap on the glass bring him into this room and leave him alone!

EDITH. (*hardly more than a nod and a whisper*)
Yes. (*turns away towards front*)

ARRELSFORD. (*goes rapidly toward door up* L., *stops
and turns near door*) I rely on you Miss Varney to
give him no hint or sign that we suspect—(*interrupted*)

(MRS. VARNEY *and* EDITH *both turn indignantly on*
ARRELSFORD. MRS. VARNEY *with slight exclamation.*)

EDITH. (C. *down a little. Interrupting* ARRELS-
FORD *on cue*) Mr. Arrelsford!

(ARRELSFORD *stands an instant—then bows stiffly
and exits at door up* L. EDITH *stands where she
was as if stunned.* MRS. VARNEY *remains* R. C.
looking after ARRELSFORD—*then turns to*
EDITH.)

EDITH. (*after pause—not looking round—nearly
whisper*) Mama! (*reaches out her hand as if feeling for help or support.* MRS. VARNEY *comes down
to* EDITH *on her left and takes her hand*) Mama!
MRS. VARNEY. (*low voice*) I'm here, Edith!

(*Pause.* EDITH *thinking of something—her eyes
wide open—staring vacantly before her.*)

EDITH. (*holding tight to* MRS. VARNEY'S *hand*)
Do you think—do you think—that could be what he
meant? (MRS. VARNEY *looking intently at* EDITH)
The Commission I got for him—this afternoon.
MRS. VARNEY. (*low voice*) Yes—yes!
EDITH. The Commission you know—from the
President—for the—for the Telegraph Service! He
—he—refused to take it!
MRS. VARNEY. Refused!
EDITH. (*nodding a little—hardly able to speak*)
He said—he said it was for me that he could not!
MRS. VARNEY. It's true then!
EDITH. (*turning quickly to* MRS. VARNEY *and try-*

*ing to stop her by putting her hand over her mouth.
Speaking rapidly, breathlessly—yet not in loud voice)*
No no! Don't say it!

MRS. VARNEY. (*putting* EDITH'*s hand away)*
Yes! .

EDITH. Oh, no!

MRS. VARNEY. Infamous traitor! They ought to
lash him through the streets of Richmond!

EDITH. (*impulsively trying to stop* MRS. VARNEY)
No Mama! No—no—no! (*she stops—a moment's
pause, she realizes the truth. Speaks in almost a
whisper*) Yes—yes—(*fainter and fainter*) Yes—
yes—(*stops—pauses—stands erect—looks about—
motions* MRS. VARNEY *to go*)

(MRS. VARNEY *turns quietly and leaves the room
going out at the door up* L. *and off* L. EDITH
*stands supporting herself without knowing that
she does so—one hand on a table or back of
chair.—Soon coming to herself she turns and
goes toward the window up* R. *When near* C. *she
stops. Stands there a moment looking toward
the window. Then brushes her hand quickly
across her eyes and takes the President's Commission from the bosom of dress. She looks at
it as if thinking, folds it slowly and puts it back
again. Walks to the window, throws aside the
curtains and pushes it open.*)

(*Upon* EDITH *pushing open the window up* R.
CAPTAIN THORNE *outside* R. *at some distance, makes sound with chair as though he
rose and pushed or set it back and the sound
of his footsteps outside approaching briskly
follows at once.* EDITH *moves back away from
the window and across to up* L. C. *near table and
stands there looking at the window up* R. *After
footsteps and after* EDITH *is motionless at
up* L. C. CAPTAIN THORNE *walks briskly and*

unsuspiciously into the room at window up R.
glancing about as he does so—not seeing EDITH
*until he is a little way, in. Upon seeing her he
stops an instant where he is, and then goes directly across to her and is about to take her
hand as he speaks.*)

THORNE. (*coming to* EDITH *up* L. C.)   Miss
Varney——

EDITH. (*as she snatches her hand away and shrinks
back slightly up* L. *Breathless*) No—don't touch
me! (*a second's pause. She recovers almost instantly*) Oh—it was you! (*smiling as if at her own
stupidity*) Why how perfectly absurd I am! (*crossing in front of* THORNE *lightly and going to window
at up* R.) Ah'm sure Ah ought to be ashamed of
myself! (*turns to him at* R.) Do come out a
minute—on the veranda—Ah want to talk to you
about a whole lot o' things! There's half an hour
yet before the party! (*turning to go*) Isn't it a
lovely night! (*she exits at the window up* R. *with
forced gaiety of manner disappearing in the darkness*) Oh, come along!

(THORNE *stands looking at* EDITH *when she first
speaks. As she crosses* R. *he is looking down a
little but looks slowly up toward front and turns
a little after her cross, looking at her as she
stands for a moment in the window up* R.
*After her exit he slowly turns toward front and
his eyes glance about and down once as he weighs
the chances.*)

EDITH. (*after brief pause for above—calling gaily
from outside up* R. *not too near the window*) Oh,
Cap'n Thorne! (*emphasis on ' oh '*)
(THORNE *turns quickly looking off* R. *again—Hesitates an instant—Makes up his mind. Walks rapidly*

to window up R.   *A very slight hesitating there—
without stopping.   Exits at window up* R.   *Ring as*
THORNE *exits*)

CURTAIN

*Time of playing—43 minutes.
Wait between Acts I and II—4 minutes.*

ACT II

SCENE:—*The same room.*

NINE O'CLOCK
_____

Furniture as in ACT I.   *Electric calciums for
strong moonlight outside both windows at* R.
Portieres are closed at both windows.
(MRS. VARNEY *discovered seated at desk* R. 1.—
*She is not busy with anything but sits watching
that no one goes out to the veranda at* R.
Sound of closing of door outside L.   *Enter* MISS
KITTRIDGE *at door up* C. *which stands ajar as
if she had recently come out.*)

MRS. VARNEY.   Was it the same man?
MISS KITTRIDGE. (*pausing up* C.)   No; they sent
another one this time.
MRS. VARNEY.   Did you have anything ready?
MISS KITTRIDGE.   Oh yes—Ah gave 'em quite a
lot.   We've all been at the bandages—that's what
they need most. (MRS. VARNEY *rises.   Seems pre-
occupied.   Goes across to* L. *and looks off.* MISS
KITTRIDGE *watches her rather anxiously a moment*)
Did you want anything, Mrs. Varney?
MRS. VARNEY. (*turning at up* L.)   No—I—nothing, thank you. (MISS KITTRIDGE *is turning to go,
but stops when* MRS. VARNEY *speaks again.* MRS.

VARNEY *goes nearer to* MISS KITTRIGE) Perhaps
it would be just as well if any of the ladies want to
go, to let them out the other way. You can open the
door into the dining-room. We're expecting someone
here on important business.

MISS KITTRIDGE. Ah'll see to it, Mrs. Varney.

MRS. VARNEY. Thank you. (*Exit* MISS KIT-
TRIDGE *at door up* C. MRS. VARNEY *stands a moment.
Then goes down* L. *and rings bell. Crosses to* R. C.,
going back of table L. C. *Then goes slowly up* C.
waiting) (*Enter* MARTHA *at door up* L. *from door* R.
of stairway. MRS. VARNEY *up* C.) Did Miss Caroline go home?

MARTHA. (*up* L. C. *near door*) No'm. She's been
out yere in de kitchen fur a while.

MRS. VARNEY. In the kitchen!

MARTHA. Yaas'm.

MRS. VARNEY. What is she doing?

MARTHA. She's been mostly sewin' and behavin'
mighty strange about sumfin a great deal o' de time.
Ah bleeve she's gittin' ready to go home now.

MRS. VARNEY. Ask her to come here a moment.

MARTHA. Yaas'm. (MARTHA *turns and exits up*
L. *and off door* R. *of stairway*) (MRS. VARNEY *waits
a little. Then goes forward* R. C. *a few steps*)
(*Enter* CAROLINE *at door up* L. *from door* R. *of
stairway. She comes into the room trying to look
very innocent*)

MRS. VARNEY. (R. C.) Caroline—(CAROLINE
goes down C. *with* MRS. VARNEY. *She is expecting
to hear something said about the sewing she has been
doing*) Are you in a hurry to get home? Because
if you can wait a few minutes while I go upstairs to
Howard it'll be a great help.

CAROLINE. (*looking around in some doubt*) You
want me to—just wait? Is that all?

MRS. VARNEY. I—(*hesitates a little*)—I don't
want anyone to go out on the veranda just now.

(CAROLINE *looks toward veranda* R.) Edith's there
—with——

CAROLINE. (*suddenly comprehending*) Oh yes!
(*glances toward windows* R.) Ah know how that is
—Ah'll attend to it! (*crosses to up* R. C.)

MRS. VARNEY. Just while I'm upstairs—it won't
be long! (*goes to door up* L. *Turns at door*) Be
careful won't you dear! (*exit at door up* L. *and up
the stairway*)

CAROLINE. (*up* R. C.) Careful!—Well Ah should
think so! As if Ah didn't know enough for that!
(*goes toward window up* R. *and pauses up* R. C. *Her
face is radiant with the imagined romance of the
situation. Peeps out slyly through curtains. After
a moment she turns, an idea having occurred to her,
and quickly rolls the lounge up across before the window. Kneels on it with her back to the audience and
tries to peep through curtains*) (*Enter* WILFRED
VARNEY *door up* L. *coming in cautiously and as if he
had been watching for an opportunity. He stops
just within the door and looks back up stairway. He
has on the trousers which* CAROLINE *fixed for him
ACT I, and also the Army Jacket—*CAROLINE *rises
and turns up* R. *from the lounge and sees* WILFRED,
*startled at first. He turns to her. She stands ador-
ing him in his uniform*)

(NOTE: *These clothes are not by any means new.—
The trousers must be all right as to length
though showing strange folds and awkwardness
at bottom from being cut off and sewed by an
amateur. But on no account must there be anything grotesque or laughable*)

CAROLINE. (*up* R. *Subdued exclamation as she
sees* WILFRED *in uniform*) Oh!

WILFRED. (L. C. *Low voice—speaking across from
door*) Mother isn't anywhere around is she?

CAROLINE. (*coming out to up* C.) She—she just went upstairs.

WILFRED. (*down* L. C. *a little*) Ah'm not running away—but if she saw me with these things on she might feel funny.

CAROLINE. (*half to herself*) She might not feel so very funny!

WILFRED. Well—you know—(*going over to desk down* R. *and taking papers and letters from pockets*) how it is with a feller's mother. (CAROLINE *nods affirmatively from up* C.) (WILFRED *business of hurriedly finding letter among others—feeling in different pockets for it—so that he speaks without much thinking what he says*) Other people don't care—but mothers—well—they're different.

CAROLINE. (C. *Speaks absently*) Yes—other people don't care! (*moves over toward up* L.—*The thought of* WILFRED *actually going gives her a slight sinking of the heart at which she herself is surprised*)

WILFRED. Ah've written that letter to the General!—Here it is—on'y Ah've got to end it off some way! (*pulls a chair sideways to desk and half sits on it—intent on finishing the letter.—Business with pen, etc. and running hand into his hair impetuously*) Ah'm not going to say " Your loving son " or any such rubbish as that! It would be an almighty letdown! Ah *love* him of course—but this isn't that kind of a letter! (*Pointing out writing on letter and speaking as if he supposed* CAROLINE *was at his shoulder*) Ah've been telling him—(*looking round sees that* CAROLINE *is standing at a considerable distance up* L. C. *looking at him*)—What's the matter?

CAROLINE. Nothing—!

WILFRED. Ah thought you wanted to help!

CAROLINE. (*quickly*) Oh yes—Ah do! Ah do! (*goes down at once to* WILFRED *at desk*)

WILFRED. (*looks in her face an instant.—Second*

or two pause) (CAROLINE *stammeringly asks*) The
—the—(*indicating his trousers by a little gesture*)
—are they how you wanted 'em?

WILFRED. What?

CAROLINE. Those things. (*pointing to trousers*
WILFRED *has on*)

WILFRED. (*glances at legs*) Oh—*they're* all right!
Fine!—Now about this letter—tell me what you
think! (*turning to letter again*)

CAROLINE. Tell me what you said!

WILFRED. Want to hear it?

CAROLINE. Ah've got to haven't I? How could
Ah help you if I didn't know what it was all about!

WILFRED. You're pretty good! (*looks at her
briefly*) You *will* help me won't you? (*catching
hold of her* R. *hand as she stands near him on his* L.)

CAROLINE. Oh' co'se Ah will—(*after an instant's
pause draws hand away from him*) about the letter!

WILFRED. That's what I mean!—It's mighty important you know! Everything depends on it!

CAROLINE. Well Ah should think so! (CAROLINE
*gets chair from up between windows and pulls it
around near* WILFRED *on his left, and sits looking
over the letter while he reads—showing deep interest*)

WILFRED. Ah just gave it to him strong!

CAROLINE. That's the *way* to give it to him!

WILFRED. You can't fool round with *him* much!
He means business! But he'll find out Ah mean
business too!

CAROLINE. That's right—everybody means business!—What did you say?

WILFRED. Ah said this!—(*reads letter*) " General Ransom Varney—Commanding Division Army
of the Northern Virginia—Dear Papa—This is to
notify you that Ah want you to let me come right
now! If you don't Ah'll come anyhow—that's all!

The eighteen call is out—the seventeen comes next an' Ah'm not going to wait for it! Do you think Ah'm a damned coward? Tom Kittridge has gone! He was killed yesterday at Cold Harbor. Billy Fisher has gone. So has Cousin Stephen and he ain't sixteen. He lied about his age but Ah don't want to do that unless you make me. Answer this right now or not at all!"

CAROLINE. That's *splendid!*

WILFRED. Do you think so?

CAROLINE. Why it's just the thing!

WILFRED. But how'm Ah going to end it?

CAROLINE. Just end it!

WILFRED. How?

CAROLINE. Sign your name.

WILFRED. Nothing else?

CAROLINE. What else is there?

WILFRED. Just " Wilfred? "

CAROLINE. O' co'se!

WILFRED. (*looks at her an instant then turns suddenly to desk and writes his name*) That's the thing! (*holds it up*) Will the rest of it do?

CAROLINE. Do! Ah should think so! (*rising*) Ah wish he had it now! (*goes toward* c.)

WILFRED. (*rising*) So do I!—It might take two or three days! (*moves toward* c.) Ah can't wait that long!—Why the Seventeen call might—(*stops. Thinks frowningly*)

CAROLINE. (*suddenly turning at* c.) Ah'll tell you what to do!—Telegraph! (WILFRED *looks at her— she at him. After an instant he glances at the letter*)

WILFRED. (c. *at* R.) Whew! (*a whistle*) Ah haven't got money enough for that!

CAROLINE. (c. *at* L.) 'Twon't take so very much!

WILFRED. Do you know what they're charging now? Over seven dollars a word!

CAROLINE. Let 'em charge! We can cut it down so there's only a few words an' it means just the same! (*they both go at the letter each holding it on his or her side*) The address won't cost a thing!

WILFRED. Won't it?

CAROLINE. No! They never do! There's a heap o' money saved right now! We can use that to pay for the rest! (WILFRED *looks at her a little puzzled*) What comes next? (*both look over the letter*)

WILFRED. (*looks at letter*) "Dear Papa"—

CAROLINE. Leave that out! (*both scratch at it with pens or pencils*)

WILFRED. Ah didn't care much for it anyway!

CAROLINE. He knew it before.

WILFRED. Ah'm glad it's out!

CAROLINE. So'm I! What's next? (*reading*) " This - is - to-notify-you-that-Ah-want-you-to-let-me-come-right-now." We might leave out that last " to."

WILFRED and CAROLINE. (*reciting it off together experimentally to see how it reads without the " to "*) " Ah-want-you—let-me-come-right-now." (*after instant's thought both shake heads*)

WILFRED. (*shaking head*) No!

CAROLINE. (*shaking head*) No!

WILFRED. It doesn't sound right.

CAROLINE. That's only a little word anyhow!

WILFRED. So it is. What's after that? (*both eagerly look at letter*)

CAROLINE. Wait—here it is! (*reads*) "If-you-don't—Ah'll—come—anyhow—that's—all." (*They consider*)

WILFRED. We might leave out " that's all."

CAROLINE. (*quickly*) No! Don't leave that out! It's very important. It doesn't seem so but it is! It shows— (*hesitates*) well—it shows that's all there is about it! That one thing might convince him!

WILFRED. We've got to leave out something!

CAROLINE. Yes—but not that! Perhaps there's something in the next! (*reads*) " The-eighteen-call-is-out—" That's got to stay!

WILFRED. (*reads*) "The-seventeen-comes-next."

CAROLINE. That's got to stay!

WILFRED. (*shaking head*) Yes!

CAROLINE. (*taking it up*) "Ah'm-not-going-to-wait-for-it!" (*shaking head without looking up*) No! No!

WILFRED. (*shaking head*) No!

CAROLINE. We'll find something in just a minute! (*reading. Wait for quiet on this—but follow in close so as not to drop*) "Do-you-think-Ah'm-a-damned-coward!" (*both look up from the letter simultaneously and gaze at each other in silence for an instant*)

WILFRED. (*after the pause*) We might leave out the——

CAROLINE. (*breaking in on him with almost a scream*) No no! (*they again regard each other*)

WILFRED. (*after the pause*) That "damn" 's going to cost us seven dollars and a half!

CAROLINE. It's worth it! Why it's the best thing you've got in the whole thing! Your papa's a general in the army! He'll *understand* that! What's next? Ah know there's something now.

WILFRED. (*reads*) "Tom-Kittridge-has-gone. He-was-killed-yesterday-at-Cold-Harbor."

CAROLINE. (*slight change in tone—a little lower*) Leave out that about his (*very slight catch of breath*) about his being killed.

WILFRED. (*looking at* CAROLINE) But he was!

CAROLINE. (*she is suddenly very quiet*) Ah know he was—but you haven't got to tell him the news—have you?

WILFRED. That's so! (*they both cross off the words*)

CAROLINE. (*becoming cheerful again*) How does it read now? (*they are both looking over the letter*)

WILFRED. It reads just the same—except that about Tom Kittridge.

CAROLINE. (*looking at* WILFRED *astonished*) Just the same! After all this work!

(*They look at one another rather astounded for an instant, then suddenly turn to the letter again and study over it earnestly. Sound of door bell in distant part of house. Soon after* MARTHA *crosses outside* L. *coming from door* R. *of stairway to go to door. Sound of door off* L. *A moment later she is seen going up the stairway carrying a large envelope.* WILFRED *and* CAROLINE *are so absorbed in work that they do not observe the bell or* MARTHA'S *movements outside up* L.)

CAROLINE. (*looking up from letter*) Everything else has *got* to stay!

WILFRED. Then we can't telegraph—it would take hundreds of dollars!

CAROLINE. (*with determination*) Yes we can! (WILFRED *looks at her. She takes the letter*) Ah'll send it! (*backing up a little toward door up* L.)

WILFRED. How can you—(*interrupted*)

CAROLINE. Never you mind!

WILFRED. (*follows her up a little*) See here! (*taking hold of the letter*) Ah'm not going to have you spending money!

CAROLINE. Ha! There's no danger! Ah haven't got any to spend!

WILFRED. (*releases hold on letter*) Then what are you going to do?

CAROLINE. (*turning up toward door up* L. *with letter*) Oh—Ah know! (*turns toward* WILFRED) Ah reckon Douglass Stafford'll send it for me!

WILFRED. (*quickly to her*) No he won't! (*they face each other.* CAROLINE *surprised*)

CAROLINE. What's the reason he won't?

WILFRED. (*slight pause*) If he wants to send it for *me* he can—but he won't send it for *you!*

CAROLINE. What do you care s' long as he sends it?

WILFRED. (*up* C. *Looking at* CAROLINE—*slight change of tone—softer*) Well—Ah care! That's enough! (*they look at each other, then both lower eyes, looking in different directions*)

CAROLINE. (*up* L. C.) Oh, well—if you feel like that about it—! (*turns away down* L. C.)

WILFRED. (*up* C. *eyes lowered*) That's the way Ah feel! (*pause*—WILFRED *looks up at her—goes down toward her*) You—you won't give up the idea of helping me because I feel like that—will you?

CAROLINE. (*impulsively, with start and turn toward* WILFRED) Mercy no—Ah'll help you all I can! (WILFRED *impulsively takes her hand as if in gratitude and so quick that she draws it away and goes on with only a slight break*) About the letter!

WILFRED. That's what Ah mean! (*they stand an instant,* CAROLINE *looking down,* WILFRED *at her*)

CAROLINE. (*suddenly turning toward desk and crossing him to* R.) Ah'm going to see if we can't leave out something else! (*sits at desk.* WILFRED *goes down* R. *near her on her* L. *and stands looking over her, intent on the letter*)

(*Enter* MRS. VARNEY, *coming down the stairway and into the room at door up* L. *She has an open letter in her hand. Also brings a belt and cap rolled up together. She pauses at the door and motions someone who is outside* L. *to come in.* MARTHA *follows her down and exits through door* R. *of stairway.*)

(*Enter an orderly up* L. *just from his horse after a long ride. Dusty, faded and bloody uniform; yellow stripes. Face sunburned and grim. He stands near the door up* L. *waiting, without effort to be precise or formal, but nevertheless being entirely soldierly.* MRS. VARNEY *waits until he enters.*)

MRS. VARNEY. (*comes down* C. *a little*) Wilfred!
(WILFRED *and* CAROLINE *turn quickly. They both
stare motionless for a moment*) Here's a letter from
your father. He sent it by the orderly. (WILFRED
moves a step or two toward MRS. VARNEY *and stands
looking at her.* CAROLINE *slowly rises with her eyes
on* MRS. VARNEY. MRS. VARNEY *speaks calmly but
with the measured quietness of one who is controlling
herself*) He tells me— (*she stops a little but it is
only her voice that falls. She does not break down
or show emotion. Holds letter toward* WILFRED)
You read it!

(WILFRED, *after glance at* CAROLINE, *steps quickly to*
   MRS. VARNEY *and takes the letter. Reads it—*
   MRS. VARNEY *looking away a little as he does
   so.* CAROLINE'S *eyes upon* WILFRED *as he reads.
   The orderly faced to* R. *on obliqued line of door.*
   WILFRED *finishes very soon—only two or three
   seconds necessary. He glances at the orderly,
   then hands the letter to his mother as he steps
   across to him.*)

WILFRED. (*standing before the orderly*)   The
General says Ah'm going back with you!
   ORDERLY. (*saluting*) His orders, sir!
   WILFRED. When do we start?
   ORDERLY. Soon as you can sir—Ah'm waiting!
   WILFRED. We'll make it right now! (WILFRED
turns and walks quickly to his mother) You won't
mind, mother.

(MRS. VARNEY *does not speak, but quietly strokes the
   hair back from his forehead with a trembling
   hand—and only once. She then hands him the
   belt and cap. Old and worn cap. Belt that
   has seen service.*)

MRS. VARNEY. (*low voice*) Your brother wanted
you to take these—I told him you were going. (WIL-

FRED *takes them. Puts on the belt at once*) He says he can get another belt—when he wants it. You're to have his blankets too—Ah'll get them. (*she crosses* WILFRED *and goes off at door up* L. *and off to* L. *going back of orderly*)

(WILFRED *finishing adjusting the belt.* CAROLINE *motionless* R. *but now looking down at the floor —facing nearly front.*)

WILFRED. (*suppresses excitement*) Fits as if it was made for me! (*to orderly*) Ah'll be with you in a jiffy! (WILFRED *goes to* CAROLINE) We won't have to send that now—(*indicating letter they have been working on*) will we? (WILFRED *stands on her* L. CAROLINE *shakes her head a little without looking up—then slowly raises left hand in which she has the letter and holds it out to him, her eyes still on the floor.* WILFRED *takes the letter mechanically and keeps it in his hand during the next few lines, tearing it up absent-mindedly*) You're pretty good—to help me like you did! You can help me again if you—if you want to! (CAROLINE *raises her eyes and looks at him*) Ah'd like to fight twice as well if— (*hesitates.* CAROLINE *looks at him an instant longer and then looks down without speaking*) Good-bye! (WILFRED *holds out his hand.* CAROLINE *puts her hand in his without looking at him*) Perhaps you'll write to me about—about helping me fight twice as well! Ah wouldn't mind if you telegraphed! That is—if you telegraphed that you would! (*slight pause.* WILFRED *holding* CAROLINE'S *hand boyishly.* CAROLINE *looking down.* WILFRED *trying to say something but not finding the words. Enter* MRS. VARNEY *at door up* L. WILFRED *hears her and turns—leaving* CAROLINE *and meeting his mother near* C. *She brings an army blanket rolled and tied.* WILFRED *takes it and slings it over his shoulder*) Good-bye mother! (*he kisses her rather*

hurriedly. MRS. VARNEY *stands passive*) You won't
mind, will you. (WILFRED *crosses at once to orderly
with eagerness and enthusiasm*) Ready sir ! (*saluting. Orderly turns and marches off at door up left.*
WILFRED *follows the orderly. Brief pause*)

(*The opening and heavy closing of the door outside
left is heard, and then it is still.* MRS. VARNEY
*is the first to move. She turns and walks slowly
up a few steps, her back to the audience, but with
no visible emotion. It is as if her eyes filled
with tears and she turned away. When* MRS.
VARNEY *stops up* C. CAROLINE *moves a little, her
eyes still down, walking slowly across toward
door left, but not with emphasized deliberation.
Merely not with her usual alacrity.* MRS. VAR-
NEY *hears her going and turns in time to speak
just before she reaches the door up* L. C.)

MRS. VARNEY. Going, dear? (CAROLINE *nods
her head a little without looking round*) Oh yes!
(*speaks with a shade of forced cheerfulness*) Your
party of course ! You ought to be there ! (CAROLINE
*stops and speaks back into the room without looking
at* MRS. VARNEY)

CAROLINE. (*subdued voice. With a sad little
shake of head*) There won't— (*shakes head again
a little*) There won't be any party to-night.
(*Exit at door up* L. *and off* L.)

MRS. VARNEY. (*after an instant's wait starts
toward door up* L.) Caroline ! Stop a moment ! (*at
door*) I don't want you to go home alone ! (*she goes
down* L. *and rings the bell*)

CAROLINE. (*outside* L.) Oh Ah don't mind !

(*Sounds of front door and heavy steps of men outside, up left.* MRS. VARNEY *goes up* L. *looks off
and then retires back a little into the room
to up* C.)

(*Enter* ARRELSFORD *and two soldiers at the door up*

L. ARRELSFORD *motions men to stand at the door
and goes quickly to* MRS. VARNEY *up* C.)

ARRELSFORD. (*low voice*) Is he—? (*a motion
toward window at* R.)

MRS. VARNEY. (*to* ARRELSFORD, *hardly above a
whisper*) Yes! (*Glances round toward window* R.)

(*Enter* CAROLINE *at door up left from off* L.)

CAROLINE. (*up* L. C.) Oh Mrs. Varney—there's
a heap o' soldiers out yere! You don't reckon anything's the mattah do you?

(*Enter* MARTHA *at door up* L. *from door* R. *of
stairway.* ARRELSFORD *goes back of* MRS. VAR-
NEY *to window up* R. *Looks through curtains
of window down* R.)

MRS. VARNEY. (*hastening to* CAROLINE) Sh!—
No—there's nothing the matter! Martha, I want
you to go home with Miss Mitford—at once! *urging*
CAROLINE *off*) Good night dear! (*kissing her*)

CAROLINE. (*up* L. C.) Good night! (*looks up in*
MRS. VARNEY'S *face*) You don't reckon she could
go with me to—(*hesitates*) somewhere else, do you?

MRS. VARNEY. (*up* L. C., R. *of* CAROLINE) Why
where do you want to go?

CAROLINE. Just to—just to the telegraph office!

(ARRELSFORD *turns sharply and looks at* CAROLINE
from window down R.)

MRS. VARNEY. Now! At this time of night!

CAROLINE. Ah've got to! Oh, it's very important
business!   .

(ARRELSFORD *down* R. *watching* CAROLINE.)

MRS. VARNEY. Of course, then Martha must go
with you! Good night!

CAROLINE. Good night! (*exit* CAROLINE *and*
MARTHA *at door up* L. *and off* L.)

Mrs. Varney. (*calling off to* Martha) Martha, don't leave her an instant!

Martha. (*outside* L. *or just going*) No'm—Ah'll take care!

(Martha *does not come into room for foregoing scene. She remains back of archway or opening up* L. C. *Heavy sound of door outside up* L.)

Arrelsford. (*going up* C. *quickly—low, sharp voice*) What is she gong to do at the telegraph office?

Mrs. Varney. (*going down* L. C. *a little. Low voice*) I've no idea! (*accent on the* "*i*")

Arrelsford. (*low voice*) Has she had any conversation with him? (*motion toward* R.)

Mrs. Varney. (*low voice*) Why—they were talking together here—early this evening! But it isn't possible she could——

Arrelsford. (*interrupting; low voice*) Anything is possible! (*goes over to* Corporal *at up* L. *quickly, passing back of* Mrs. Varney. Mrs Varney *moves to up* R. C. *as* Arrelsford *crosses at back*) Have Eddinger follow that girl! Don't let any dispatch go out until I see it! Make no mistake about that! (Corporal *exits with salute at door up* L. *and off* L. *Brief pause.* Arrelsford *turns to* Mrs. Varney) Are they both out there? (*motions toward* R.)

Mrs. Varney. (*up* R. C. *Low tone. A glance back at* R. *first*) Yes! Did you bring the man from Libby Prison.

Arrelsford. (L. *of her. Low voice*) The guard's holding him in the street. When we get Thorne in here alone I'll have him brought up to that window (*pointing at window up* R.) an' shoved into the room!

(Corporal *re-appears at the door up* L. *and waits for further orders.* Arrelsford *and* Mrs. Varney *continue in low tones*)

Mrs. Varney. (R. C.) Where shall I——

Arrelsford. Out there (*pointing up* L. *and going toward door a little*) where you can get a view of this room!

Mrs. Varney. But if he sees me——

Arrelsford. He won't if it's dark in the hall! (*turns to* Corporal *and gives order in low distinct voice*) Shut off those lights out there! (*indicating lights outside the door or archway up left.* Corporal *exits up* L. *Lights off*) We can close these curtains can't we?

Mrs. Varney. Yes. (Arrelsford *draws curtains at door or archway up* L.)

Arrelsford. I don't want much light in here! (*indicating drawing-room.* Corporal *and* Men *exit up Left*)

(Arrelsford *goes to table up* L. C. *and turns gas or lamp down.* Mrs. Varney *turns down lamp on desk* R. 1.—*Stage in half light.*)

Arrelsford. (*carefully moves couch away from window up* R. *and opens portieres of window.— Almost in a whisper*) Now open those curtains! Carefully! Don't attract attention! (*indicating window down* R.)

(Mrs. Varney *very quietly draws back the curtains to window down* R. *Moonlight on through window down* R. *covering as much of stage as possible. Moonlight also strong on backing up* R.)

Arrelsford. (*moving over to up* L. C. *Speaking across to* Mrs. Varney *after the lights are down*) Are those women in there yet? (*indicating door up* C.)

Mrs. Varney. Yes.

Arrelsford. Where's the key? (Mrs. Varney *moves noiselessly to the door up* C.) Is it on the inside?

(Mrs. Varney *turns and nods affirmatively.*)

Arrelsford. Lock the door!

(Mrs. Varney *turns the key as noiselessly as possible.* Edith *suddenly appears at window up* R. *coming on quickly and closing the windows after her.*—Mrs. Varney *and* Arrelsford *both turn and stand looking at her.*—Edith *turns to them and stands an instant.*)

Edith. (*going down* R. C. *and stretching out left hand toward* Mrs. Varney—*Very low voice—but breathlessly and with intensity*) Mama! (Mrs. Varney *hurries forward with her* C. Edith *on her* R. Arrelsford *remains up* L. C. *looking on*) I want to speak to you!

Arrelsford. (L. C. *Low tone—Stepping forward*) We can't wait!

Edith. (C.) You must! (Arrelsford *moves back protestingly.* Edith *turns to* Mrs. Varney—*Almost a whisper*) I can't—I can't do it! Oh—let me go!

Mrs. Varney. (C. *Very low voice*) Edith! You were the one who——

Edith. (*almost a whisper*) I was sure then!

Mrs. Varney. Has he confessed?

Edith. (*quickly*) No no! (*glance toward* Arrelsford)

Arrelsford. (*low voice—sharp*) Don't speak so loud!

Mrs. Varney. (*low voice*) What is it Edith—You must tell me!

Edith. (*almost a whisper*) Mama—he loves me! (*breathless with emotion*)—Yes—and I——Oh—let someone else do it!

Mrs. Varney. You don't mean that you— (Arrelsford *comes forward quickly* L. C.)

EDITH. (*seeing* ARRELSFORD *approach and crossing* MRS. VARNEY *to him*) No no! Not now! Not now!

MRS. VARNEY. (C. R. *Low voice*) More reason now than ever!

ARRELSFORD. (C. L. *Low voice*) We *must* go on!

EDITH. (C. *Turning desperately upon* ARRELSFORD. *Low voice*) Why are you doing this?

ARRELSFORD. (*low voice*) Because I please!

EDITH. (*low voice—but with force*) You never pleased before! Hundreds of suspicious cases have come up—hundreds of men have been run down—but you preferred to sit at your desk in the War Department.

MRS. VARNEY. (*low voice*) Edith!

ARRELSFORD. (*low voice*) We won't discuss that now!

EDITH. (*low voice*) No—we'll end it! I'll have nothing more to do with the affair!

ARRELSFORD. (*low voice*) You won't!

MRS. VARNEY. (*low voice*) You won't!

EDITH. (*low voice*) Nothing at all!—Nothing!—Nothing!

ARRELSFORD. (*low voice but with vehemence*) At your own suggestion Miss Varney, I agreed to a plan by which we could criminate this friend of yours—or establish his innocence. At the critical moment—when everything's ready you propose to withdraw—making it a failure and perhaps allowing him to escape altogether!

MRS. VARNEY. (*low voice*) You mustn't do this Edith!

EDITH. (*low voice—But desperately*) He's there! The man is there—at the further end of the veranda! What more do you want of me!

ARRELSFORD. (*low voice. Sharp. Intense*) Call 'im into this room! If anyone else should do it he'd suspect! He'd be on his guard!

EDITH. (*after pause. Low voice*) Very well—I'll call 'im into this room. (*moves as if to do so*)

ARRELSFORD. (*low voice*) One thing more! I want 'im to have this paper! (*holding out paper that was taken from* JONAS *in* ACT I) Tell 'im where it came from—tell 'im the old niggah got it from a prisoner in Libby!

EDITH. (*quietly. Low voice*) Why am I to do this?

ARRELSFORD. (*low but very strong*) Why not? If he's innocent where's the harm?—If not—if he's in this plot—the message on that paper will send 'im to the telegraph office to-night and that's just where we want him!

EDITH. (*low voice*) I never promised that!

ARRELSFORD. (*hard sharp voice though subdued*) Do you still believe him innocent?

(*Pause.* EDITH *slowly raises her head erect. Looks* ARRELSFORD *full in the face.*)

EDITH. (*almost whisper*) I still—believe him—innocent!

ARRELSFORD. Then why are you afraid to give him this? (*indicating paper*)

(*Pause.* EDITH *turns to* ARRELSFORD. *Stretches out her hand for the paper.*—ARRELSFORD *puts the paper in* EDITH'S *hand. She pauses a moment.*—ARRELSFORD *and* MRS. VARNEY *watch her. She turns and moves up a few steps toward the window. Stops and stands listening up* C. *Noise of chair off* R.)

EDITH. (*low voice*) Captain Thorne's coming.

ARRELSFORD. (*going to door up* L. C. *and holding curtain back*) This way Mrs. Varney! Quick! Quick! (ARRELSFORD *and* MRS. VARNEY *hasten off at the door up* L. *closing portieres after them*)

(EDITH *moves down* L. C. *and stands near table.—
Sound of* THORNE'S *footsteps on veranda outside
windows* R.—EDITH *slowly turns toward the
window up* R. *and stands looking at it with a
fascinated dread.* THORNE *opens the window
up* R. *and enters at once, coming a few steps into
the room, when he stops and stands an instant
looking at* EDITH *as she looks strangely at him.
Then he goes to her.*)

THORNE. (*low voice—near* EDITH) Is anything
the matter?

EDITH. (*slightly shakes her head before speaking.
Nearly a whisper*) Oh no! (*emphasize " no."
Stands looking up in his face*)

THORNE. (*low voice*) You've been away such
a long time!

EDITH. (*low voice*) Only a few minutes!

THORNE. (*low voice*) Only a few years.

EDITH. (*easier*) Oh—if that's a few years—(*turning away front a little*) what a lot of time there is!

THORNE. (*low voice*) No.—There's only to-night!

EDITH. (*turning to him. A breathless interrogation*) What!

THORNE. (*taking her hands*) There's only to-night and you in the world!—Oh—see what I've been doing! I came here determined not to tell you I love you—and for the last half hour I've been telling you nothing else! Ah, my darling—there's only to-night and you!

EDITH. (*suddenly moving back a little from him.
Nearly a breathless whisper*) No no—you mustn't!
(*a quick apprehensive glance around down toward
left and back*)—not now! (EDITH *speaks the above
very fast—and as if afraid she would be overheard.
She stands turned away from him to front*)

(THORNE *holds position he was in an instant. Then
moves back slightly, and as she is looking front*

*he darts a quick suspicious glance toward cur-
tains up L. and instantly back to her.* EDITH
moves forward a little, THORNE *slowly releasing
her hand.—After looking at her there an instant*
THORNE *darts another swift glance—this time
toward the window up* R. *and the same instant
back to her again.*)

THORNE. (*low voice. From where he stands—
above her*) Don't mind what I said Miss Varney—
I must have forgotten myself. (*brief pause. He
steps down to right of* EDITH) Believe me I came
to make a friendly call and—and say good-bye.
(*bowing slightly*) Permit me to do so now. (*turns
up at once making turn to* L. *and walks toward door
up Left*)

EDITH. (*quickly across to* R. C. *as* THORNE *goes
up*) Oh!—Cap'n Thorne! (*this is timed to stop*
THORNE *just before he reaches the closed portieres of
door up* L. THORNE *turns up* L. C. *and looks at*
EDITH. *Calcium across from window* R. *on him.*
EDITH *trying to be natural—but her lightness somewhat forced*) Before you go I—(*slight quiver in
her voice*)—I wanted to ask your advice about something! (*she stands turned a little to front*)

(THORNE *looks at her motionless an instant longer,
then turns his head slowly toward the portieres
on his left. Turns back to* EDITH *at* R. C. *again
and at once moves down to her on her* L.)

THORNE. (*as he comes down to* EDITH) Yes?
EDITH. (*a little* R. *of* C.) What do you think
this means? (*holds the piece of paper out toward
him but avoids looking in his face*)
THORNE. (L. *of* EDITH. *Stepping quickly to her
and taking the paper easily*) Why, what is it? (*a
half-glance at the paper as he takes it*)
EDITH. It's a—(*hesitates slightly. Recovers at*

once and looks up at him brightly) That's what I want you to tell me.

THORNE. *(looking at the paper)* Oh—you don't know!

EDITH. *(shaking her head slightly)* No. *(stands waiting—eyes averted)* (THORNE *glances quickly at her an instant on peculiar tone of " no ")*

THORNE. *(looking again at the paper)* A note from someone?

EDITH. It might be.

THORNE. *(glancing about)* Well, it's pretty dark here! *(glances* R. *toward low-turned lamp on desk. Crosses to it)* If you'll excuse me I'll turn up this lamp a little more—*(going* R. *to desk)* then we can see what it is. *(turns up lamp. Lights on foots 1-2)* There we are! *(looks at paper. As soon as he sees it, looks front quickly showing that he recognizes it. But no start. Slow turn to* EDITH. *Then looks at the paper again—Reads as if with difficulty)* " Attack . . . . to-night " . . . . There's something about " Attack to-night "—*(turns to* EDITH) Could you make out what it was?

(EDITH *shakes head negatively. Her lips move, but she cannot speak. She turns away.)*

(THORNE *looks at her a second—then a slow turn of head, looking up stage—then turns to examine the paper again)* " Attack . . . . to-night . . . . plan . . . . three." *(Looks up to front as if considering. Repeats)* Plan three! *(Considering again—slight laugh)* Well—this thing must be a puzzle of some kind, Miss Varney. *(Turning to* EDITH)

EDITH. *(slowly. Strained voice, as if forcing herself to speak)* It was taken from a Yankee prisoner!

THORNE. *(instantly coming from former easy altitude into one showing interest and surprise. Look-*

ing at EDITH) So!—Yankee prisoner eh? (*while speaking he is instinctively holding paper in right hand as if to look at it again when he finishes speaking to* EDITH)

EDITH. Yes—down in Libby!—He gave it to one of our servants—old Jonas!

THORNE. (*turns quickly to paper*) Why here! This might be something— (*Looks again at the paper*) " Attack to-night—plan three—use Telegraph—" (*second's pause. He looks up front*) Use telegraph! (*turns quickly to* EDITH *and goes toward her*) This might be something important Miss Varney! Looks like a plot on our Department Telegraph Lines! Who did Jonas give it to?

EDITH. No one!

THORNE. Well—how—how—(*interrupted*)

EDITH. We took it away from him!

THORNE. Oh! (*long ' Oh ' of ' How could you.' Starting at once as if to cross above* EDITH *to* L.) That was a mistake!

EDITH. (*detaining him. Speaks rapidly—almost a whisper*) What are you going to do?

THORNE. (*strong. Determined*) Find that nigger and make him tell who this paper was for—he's the man we want! (*crossing back of her to* L. *and up toward door*)

EDITH. (*turning quickly to him*) Cap'n Thorne— they've lied about you!

THORNE. (*wheeling round like a flash—and coming down quickly* L. *of her*) Lied about me! What do you mean? (*seizing her hands and looking in her face to read what it is*)

EDITH. (*quick—breathless—very low—almost whisper*) Don't be angry—I didn't think it would be like this!

THORNE. (*with great force*) Yes—but what have you done?

EDITH. (*breaking loose from him and crossing to*

L.) No! (*almost a quick cry spoken close on his speech*)

THORNE. (*as she crosses before him—trying to detain her*) But I must know!

(*Heavy sound of door outside* L. *and of steps and voices in the hall—' Here! This way!' etc.*)

CORPORAL. (*off* L. *Speaking outside door up* L.) This way! Look out on that side will you?

(THORNE *stands near* C. *listening.*)

EDITH. Oh! (*going rapidly up* L.)—I don't want to be here! (*she exits door up* L. *and goes up stairs out of the way of the soldiers.* THORNE *instantly backs down to* R. *of* C. *drawing revolver and stands ready for attack from up* L.)

(*Enter at once on exit of* EDITH, CORPORAL *with two men at door up* L. *They cross rapidly toward window up* R.—CORPORAL *leading, carrying a lighted lantern.* THORNE, *seeing* CORPORAL, *at once breaks position and moves across towards up* C. *as men cross, watching* CORPORAL *who is up* R. C.)

CORPORAL. (*near window up* R.) Out here! Look out now!

(*The men exit at window up* R.)

THORNE. (*quick on* CORPORAL'S *speech so as to stop him at* R. C.) What is it Corporal? (*putting revolver back into holster*)

(THORNE *stands up* C. *in light of calcium from window up* R. *facing* CORPORAL R.)

CORPORAL. (*turning at up* R. *and saluting*) Prisoner sir—broke out o' Libby! We've run him down the street—he turned in here somewhere! If he comes in that way would you be good enough to let us know! (*pointing to the window down* R.)

THORNE. Go on, Corporal! (*starts across to window down* R.) I'll look out for this window!

(*Exit* CORPORAL *window up* R.)

(THORNE *strides rapidly to window down* R.—*Pushes curtains back each side and stands within the window looking off. Right hand on revolver.* L. *hand holding curtains back. Moonlight on through window down* R. *across stage and also from window up* R. *Dead pause for an instant. Suddenly the two men who crossed with* COR-PORAL *appear at window up* R. *holding* HENRY DUMONT. *With a sudden movement they force him on through the window and disappear quickly outside off to* R. DUMONT *stands where he landed up* R. C. *looking back through window not comprehending what is going on. He gives a quick glance about the room.* DUMONT *wears uniform of United States Cavalry, worn with service. He is pale as from lack of food— but not emaciated or ill. Hold this Tableau:—* THORNE *down* R. *standing motionless near window waiting—*DUMONT *up* R. C., *holding position he struck on entrance. Enough light on him to show the blue United States uniform. After a second's pause* DUMONT *turns from the window and looks slowly about the room, taking in the various points like a caged animal, turning his head very slowly as he looks one way and another. Soon he moves a few steps down* R. C. *and pauses. Turns and makes out a doorway up* L., *and after a glance round, he walks rapidly toward it. Just before he reaches the door there is a slight sound outside, and the blades of two or three bayonets come down into position through the curtains,*

showing at the door and barring his exit. He
*stops on seeing the bayonets. Slight click of
bayonets striking together as they come into position. Set light outside window* R. *to strike
across on blades of bayonets.*)

(*On noise of bayonets up* L. THORNE *turns quickly
and moves a few steps into the room, trying to
see who is there. He sees* DUMONT *up* L. *and
stands looking across at him. Bayonets withdrawn at once after they are shown.* DUMONT
*turns from the door and begins to move slowly
down stage at* L., *along the wall. Just as he is
coming around table down* L. *toward* C. *he sees*
THORNE *and stops dead. Both men motionless,
their eyes upon each other. Hold it several
seconds.* DUMONT *makes a start as if to escape
through window up* R., *moving across toward it.*)

THORNE. (*quick and loud order as* DUMONT *starts
toward window*) Halt!—You're a prisoner!

(DUMONT, *after instant's hesitation on* THORNE'S
order, starts rapidly toward window up R.
THORNE *heads him off, meeting him up* R. C. *and
seizes him.*)

THORNE. (*as he heads* DUMONT *off*) Halt! I
say!

(*The two men struggle together, moving quickly
down stage to* L. C., *very close to front—getting as far as possible from those who are
watching them.*)

THORNE. (*loud voice, as they struggle down stage*)
here's your man Corporal! What are you doing
there?

DUMONT. (*when down as far as possible—holding* THORNE *motionless an instant and hissing out between his teeth, without pause or inflection on words*) ATTACK TO-NIGHT—PLAN THREE —TELEGRAPH—DO YOU GET IT?

THORNE. (*quick on it*) YES!

(*This dialogue in capitals shot at each other with great force and rapidity—and so low that people outside door up* L. *could not hear.*)

DUMONT. (*low voice—almost whisper*) They're watching us! Shoot me in the leg!

THORNE. (*holding* DUMONT *motionless*) No no! I can't do that!

DUMONT. You must!

THORNE. (*quick on it*) I can't shoot my own brother!

DUMONT. It's the only way to throw 'em off the scent!

THORNE. Well I won't do it anyhow!

DUMONT. If you won't do it I will! Give me that revolver! (*pushing left arm out to get revolver*)

THORNE. (*holding* DUMONT'S *arm back motionless*) No no Harry! You'll hurt yourself!

DUMONT. (*beginning struggle to get revolver*) I don't care! Let me have it! (*etc., as they struggle up* C.)

(*They struggle quickly up* C. *a little to* R.—*so that they are in light from window down* R.)

THORNE. (*calling out as he struggles up* C. *with* DUMONT) Here's your man Corporal! What's the matter with you!

DUMONT. (*holding* THORNE *motionless up* C. *in light and trying to get at his revolver*) Give me that gun!

THORNE. (*as* DUMONT *holds him up* C. *and is just getting revolver*) (*Loud—aspirated—sharp!*) Look out Harry! You'll hurt yourself! (*Gets his* R. *hand on revolver to hold it*) (DUMONT *manages with his* L. *to wrench* THORNE'S *hand loose from the revolver and hold it up while he seizes the weapon with his* R. *hand and pulls it out of the holster. At the same time he shoves* THORNE *off to* R.)

THORNE. (*as* DUMONT *throws him off* R.) Look out! (*this follows right on last speech ' hurt yourself'*). (DUMONT *moves back to up* C. *attempting to fire the gun at himself. Before* THORNE *can recover and turn at right* DUMONT *fires. There is a quick sharp scream from ladies outside* L. DUMONT *with a groan, staggers down toward* C. *and falls mortally wounded holding the revolver in his hand until he is down and then releasing it, so that* THORNE *can find it near.*)

THORNE. (*back against chair at* R.*—which he was flung against and nearly upset. On shot and scream*) Harry—you've shot yourself! (*instantly on this he dives for the revolver that* DUMONT *has dropped and gets it, coming up on same motion with it in right hand and stands in careless attitude just over* DUMONT'S *body to* R. *of it. Men's voices heard outside up* L. ARRELSFORD *giving an order*)

(*Enter* ARRELSFORD *and men from door up left, followed by* EDITH, MRS. VARNEY *and* MISS KITTRIDGE.—*Enter* CORPORAL *and men from the window up* R. ARRELSFORD *runs at once to table up* C. *and turns up lamp. Others stand on tableau—*MRS. VARNEY *and* EDITH *at left* MISS KITTRIDGE *up* L. *Men in doorway and up* R. C.*—near window.* ARRELSFORD'S *cue to enter is* THORNE'S *getting revolver. Others on with him, with quick exclamations as below, and* *stand at once on tableau—so that* THORNE'S *line comes right on their entrance and lights up and all quiet.)*

(*Lights full on instantly on* ARRELSFORD *reaching lamp. Should come nearly on entrance of people*)

ARRELSFORD, MRS. VARNEY, EDITH, MISS KITTRIDGE, CORPORAL, MEN. (*as they enter*) Where is he! What has he done! He's shot the man! This way now! (*etc. etc. These different exclamations nearly together as they rush into the room*).

(*Exclamations stop at once on lights on.*)

THORNE. (*with careless swing of revolver across him toward c. as he brings it up to put back into holster—as the people stop quiet*) There's your prisoner Corporal—look out for him! (*stands at* R. C. *putting revolver back into holster*)

CURTAIN

Time of playing—22 minutes.
Wait between Acts II and III—9 minutes.

ACT III

SCENES:—*The War Department Telegraph Office.*
TEN O'CLOCK

Plain and somewhat battered and grimy room. Stained and smoky walls. Large windows—the glass covered with grime and cobwebs. Plaster off walls and ceiling in some places. All this from neglect—not from bombardment. It is a room in a public building which was formerly somewhat handsome. Moldings and stucco-work broken and discolored.

It is on the second floor of the building.

Very large and high door or double doors up R. C. *obliqued. This door opens to a corridor showing plain corridor-backing of a public building. This door must lead off well to* R. *so that it shall not interfere with window showing street up* L. C. *Three wide French windows up* L. C. *obliqued a little—opening down to floor, with balcony outside extending* R. *and* L. *and showing several massive white columns, bases at balcony and extending up out of sight as if for several stories above. Part of the building with columns shown in perspective, as if a wing. Backing of windows showing night view of city roofs and buildings as from height of second floor. Large disused fireplace with elaborate marble mantel in bad repair and very dirty on* R. *side behind telegraph tables. Door up* C. *opening to cupboard with shelves on which are Battery Jars and Telegraph Office truck of various kinds. Room lighted by gas on* R. *to turn out easily on stage. Show evening through window up* L.—*dark, with lights of buildings very faint and distant, keeping general effect outside window of darkness—to avoid distracting attention from interior of room. Electric Calciums (moonlight) to throw on at window on cues and also hold it on the massive white columns—and on the characters who go out on the balcony. Corridor outside door up* R. C. *not strongly illuminated. In the room itself fair light but not brilliant. Plain, solid table with telegraph instruments down*

R. C. *Other tables with instruments along wall at right side. Table down* R. C. *braced to look as if fastened securely to the floor. Also see that wire connections are properly made from all the instruments in the room to wires running up the wall on right side, thence across along ceiling to up* L. *and out through broken lights in upper part of windows up* L. *This large bunch of wires leading out, in plain sight, is most important. Large office clock over mantel set at 10 o'clock at opening and to run without fail during the Act.*

Two instruments A. *and* D. *on table down* R. C.— A. *is at* R. *end of table and is only one used at that table,* D. *being for safety.* B. *and* C. *on long table against fireplace.* B. *is at lower end of table.* C. *at upper end; one chair at table down* R. C. *Two chairs at table* R. *One chair up* C. *No sound of cannonading in this Act.*

(*At opening there are two operators at work, one at table down* R. C. *one at one of the tables on* R. *side. They are in old gray uniforms, but in shirt sleeves. Coats are hung up or thrown on chairs one side. Give busy click-effects of instruments—but do not over-do it. After first continued clicking for a moment there are occasional pauses. Messengers* A. *and* B. *near door up* R. C. *Messenger No. 3 in front of door* C. *talking to messenger No. 4 Messenger No. 2 looking out of middle window over* L.)

SECOND OPERATOR. (LIEUT. ALLISON) (*At table* R. *instrument* B. *finishing writing a dispatch*) Ready here! (*Messenger* A. *steps quickly forward and takes dispatch*) Department! The Secretary must have it to-night! (MESSENGER *salutes and*

*exits quickly at door up 'R. with dispatch. Short
pause. Other* MESSENGER *standing on attention)*

FIRST OPERATOR. (LIEUT. FORAY) (*At table down
R. C. instrument A.*) Ready here! (MESSENGER B.—
steps quickly down and takes dispatch from FIRST
OPERATOR) To the President—General Watson—
marked private! (MESSENGER B., *salutes and off
quickly door up* R.)

(*Business continues a short time as before. Second*
OPERATOR *at* R. *moves to another instrument
when it begins to click and answers call*)

(MESSENGER 1. *enters hurriedly at door up* R. *and
comes down* L. *of table* R. C. *with dispatch.*)

MESSENGER 1. Major Bridgman!
FIRST OPERATOR. (*looking up from work*)
Bridgman! Where's that?
MESSENGER 1. (*glances at dispatch*) Long-
street's Corp.
FIRST OPERATOR. That's yours Allison. (*resumes
work at instrument* A.)

(SECOND OPERATOR *holds out hand for dispatch.*
MESSENGER 1 *crosses back of table* R. C. *gives it
to him and exits at door up* R. *Bus. continues as
before.* SECOND OPERATOR *sends message on in-
instrument* B. *Sound of band of music in distance beginning very pp. increasing very gradually.* MESSENGERS *go to windows up* L. *and
look out but glance now and then at operators.*)

MESSENGER 2. (*opening* C. *window and looking
out while music is coming on and still distant*)
What's that going up Main Street?
MESSENGER 3. (*looks out*) Richmond Grays!
MESSENGERS 2 and 4. (*together*) No!

(*All look out through middle window up* L.)

MESSENGER 2. That's what they are, sure enough!

MESSENGER 3. They're sending 'em down the river!

MESSENGER 2. Not to-night!

MESSENGER 4. Seems like they was, though!

MESSENGER 3. I didn't reckon they'd send the Grays out without there was something going on!

MESSENGER 4. How do you know but what there is?

MESSENGER 2. To-night! Why good God! It's as quiet as a tomb!

MESSENGER 4. Ah reckon that's what's worrying 'em! It's so damned unusual!

(*Sound of band gradually dies away. Before music dies away,* FIRST OPERATOR *finishes a dispatch from instrument* A. *and calls.*)

FIRST OPERATOR. Ready here! (MESSENGER 3. *down to him to* L. *of table* R. C. *and takes dispatch*) Department—from General Lee—duplicate to the President!

(MESSENGER 3 *salutes and exits quickly up* R. *Business goes on. Enter an* ORDERLY, *door up* R. *Goes quickly down to* FIRST OPERATOR. MESSENGERS 2 *and* 4 *stand, talking near windows* L.)

ORDERLY. (L. *of table* R. C. *salutes*) The Secretary wants to know if there's anything from General Lee come in to-night?

FIRST OPERATOR. Just sent one over an' a duplicate went out to the President.

ORDERLY. The President's with the Cabinet yet— he didn't go home! They want an operator right quick to take down a cipher.

FIRST OPERATOR. (*calling out to* SECOND OPERATOR) Got anything on, Charlie?

SECOND OPERATOR. Not right now!

FIRST OPERATOR. Well go over to the Department—they want to take down a cipher.

(SECOND OPERATOR *gets coat and exits door up* R. *putting coat on as he goes, followed by the* ORDERLY *who came for him. Business and click of instruments goes on. Door up* R. *is opened from outside by a couple of young officers in showy and untarnished uniforms, who stand in most polite attitudes waiting for a lady to pass in.* FIRST OPERATOR *very busy writing at table* R. C. *taking message from instrument* A *but stops this message for* CAROLINE *scene.*)

FIRST YOUNG OFFICER. Right this way, Miss Mitford!

SECOND YOUNG OFFICER. Allow me, Miss Mitford! This is the Department Telegraph office!

(*Enter at the door up* R. CAROLINE MITFORD. *The young officers follow her in.* MARTHA *enters after the officers, and waits near door well up stage.*)

CAROLINE. (*coming down* C. *as she comes in, speaks in rather subdued manner and without vivacity, as if her mind were upon what she came for— hardly giving a thought to the young officers*) Thank you!

FIRST YOUNG OFFICER. (*on her* L.) Ah'm afraid you've gone back on the Army, Miss Mitford!

(CAROLINE *looks at* FIRST YOUNG OFFICER *questioningly.*)

CAROLINE. (C.) Gone where?

SECOND YOUNG OFFICER. (*on* CAROLINE'S R.) Seems like we ought to a' got a salute as you went by!

CAROLINE. Oh yes! (*salutes in perfunctory and absent-minded manner and turns away glancing about room and moving down a step or two*) Good evening! (*nodding to one of the* MESSENGER'S *waiting up* L. C.)

MESSENGER 2. (*touching cap and stepping quickly to* CAROLINE L. *of* FIRST YOUNG OFFICER) Good evening, Miss Mitford! Could we do anything for you in the office to-night?

(MESSENGER A. *remains up near upper window* L.)

CAROLINE. Ah want to send a telegram!

(*The three officers stand looking at* CAROLINE *quieted for a moment by her serious tone.*)

SECOND YOUNG OFFICER. Ah'm afraid you've been havin' bad news, Miss Mitford?

CAROLINE. (C.) No— (*shaking her head*) no!

FIRST YOUNG OFFICER. (L. C.) Maybe some friend o' yours has gone down to the front!

CAROLINE. (*beginning to be interested*) Well— supposing he had—would you call that bad news?

FIRST YOUNG OFFICER. Well Ah didn't know as you'd exactly like to——

CAROLINE. Then let me tell you—as you didn't know—that *all* my friends go down to the front!

SECOND YOUNG OFFICER. I hope not *all* Miss Mitford!

CAROLINE. Yes—all! If they didn't they wouldn't *be* my friends.

FIRST YOUNG OFFICER. But some of us are obliged to stay back here to take care of you.

CAROLINE. Well there's altogether too many trying to take care of me! You're all discharged! (*crosses to* L. *corner*)

(MESSENGER NO. 3 *enters door up* R. C. *and joins*

MESSENGER No. 4 *up* L. C. *near upper window.*
Officers fall back a little, looking rather foolish
but entirely good-natured.)

SECOND YOUNG OFFICER. (C. *good-naturedly*)
If we're really discharged Miss Mitford, looks like
we'd have to go!

FIRST YOUNG OFFICER. (L. C.) Yes—but we're
mighty sorry to see you in such bad spirits Miss
Mitford!

SECOND YOUNG OFFICER and MESSENGER 2. L. C.
and C. *together*) Yes indeed we are, Miss Mitford!

CAROLINE. (L. *turning*) Would you like to put
me in real good spirits?

FIRST YOUNG OFFICER. Would we!

SECOND YOUNG OFFICER. You try us once!

MESSENGER 2. Ah reckon there ain't anything
we'd like bettah!

CAROLINE. (L.) Then Ah'll tell you *just* what to
do! (*they listen eagerly*) Start out this very night
and never stop till you get to where my friends are—
lying in trenches and ditches and earthworks between
us and the Yankee guns!

SECOND YOUNG OFFICER, FIRST YOUNG OFFICER,
MESSENGER 2. (*remonstrating*) But really, Miss—
you don't mean—(etc.)

CAROLINE. Fight Yankees a few days and lie in
ditches a few nights till those uniforms you've got
on look like they'd been some *use* to somebody! If
you're so mighty anxious to do something for me,
that's what you can do! (*turning away to* L.) It's
the only thing Ah want!

(*The young officers stand rather discouraged an in-*
stant L. C.)

FIRST OPERATOR. (*business*) Ready here!
(MESSENGER 3 *steps quickly down to* L. *of table* R. C.)

Department! Commissary General's office! (MES-
SENGER 3 *salutes, takes dispatch and exits up* R. C.
MESSENGER 2 *returns to* MESSENGR 4 *during this,
and stands with him near window up* L. C.)

(MESSENGER A. *enters quickly at door up* R. C. *and
   comes down to* OPERATOR 1, L. *of table* R. C.
   *handing him a dispatch and at once makes his
   exit again doors* R. C. FIRST *and* SECOND
   YOUNG OFFICERS *exit dejectedly at door up* R. C.
   after this MESSENGER.)

CAROLINE. (*going across with determined air to*
R. C. *near* OPERATOR 1 *when she sees an opportunity*)
Oh Lieutenant Foray! (*accent on "Oh"*)

FIRST OPERATOR. (*turns and rises quickly with
half salute.* CAROLINE *gives a little attempt at a
military salute*) I beg your pardon, Miss! (*grabs
at his coat which is on a chair or table near at* R.
and hastily starts to put it on) I didn't know——

CAROLINE. (*up* C. *a little. Remonstrating*) No
no—don't! Ah don't mind. You see—Ah came on
business!

FIRST OPERATOR. (*puts on coat*) Want to send
something out?

CAROLINE. Yes!

FIRST OPERATOR. (*going to her, crossing back of
table* R. C.) 'Fraid we can't do anything for you
here! This is the War Department, Miss.

CAROLINE. Ah know that—but it's the on'y way
to send, an' Ah—(*sudden loud click of instrument on
instrument* B. *Table* R. FIRST OPERATOR *turns and
listens*)

FIRST OPERATOR. (*crossing back of table* R. C.)
Excuse me a minute, won't you? (*going to instrument on lower table* R. *and answering. Writing
down message, etc.*)

CAROLINE. Yes—Ah will. (*a trifle disconcerted,
stands uneasily up* C.)

FIRST OPERATOR. Ready here! (MESSENGER 2 *down quickly to* L. *of* FIRST OPERATOR *at table* R.) Department! Quick as you can—they're waiting for it! (MESSENGER 2 *takes dispatch—salutes and exits at door up* R. FIRST OPERATOR *rises and crosses to* CAROLINE *who is up* C. *To* CAROLINE) Now what was it you wanted us to do, Miss?

CAROLINE. (C.) Just to (*short gasp*) to send a telegram.

FIRST OPERATOR. (R. C.) I reckon it's private business?

CAROLINE. (C. *Looking at him with wide open eyes*) Ye—yes! It's—private!

FIRST OPERATOR. Then you'll have to get an order from some one in the department. (*goes down to back of table* R. C. *and picks up papers*)

CAROLINE. That's what Ah thought (*taking out a paper*) so Ah got it. (*hands it to* OPERATOR)

FIRST OPERATOR. (*glancing at paper*) Oh— Major Selwin!

CAROLINE. Yes—he—he's one of my——

FIRST OPERATOR. It's all right then! (*instrument* B. *calls. Quickly picks up a small sheet of paper and a pen and places them on table* L. C. *near* CAROLINE *and pushes chair up with almost the same movement*) You can write it here Miss. (*this is on upper side of the telegraph table down* R. C.)

CAROLINE. Thank you. (*sits at table—looks at small sheet of paper—picks out large sheet—smooths it out. Business of writing*)

(FIRST OPERATOR *returns to table at down* R. *and answers call and sits—writes hurriedly, taking down dispatch.* CAROLINE *earnestly writing— pausing an instant to think once or twice and a nervous glance toward* FIRST OPERATOR. FIRST OPERATOR *very busy.* MARTHA *standing motionless up stage, waiting—her eyes fixed on the*

telegraph instruments. CAROLINE *bus. of start
and drawing away suspiciously on loud click of
instrument* A. *near her. Moves over to* L. *side
of table, looking suspiciously at the instrument—
puts pen in mouth—gets ink on tongue—makes
wry face.* CAROLINE *carefully folds up her
despatch when she has written it, and turns
down a corner.* FIRST OPERATOR *when nearly
through, motions to* MESSENGER 4 *and speaks
hurriedly.*)

FIRST OPERATOR. (*still writing*) Here! (MES-
SENGER 4 *comes down quickly* L. *of* FIRST OPERATOR
and business) Department! Try to get it in before the President goes! (*handing* MESSENGER 4
dispatch. MESSENGER 4 *salutes and exits at door
up* R. FIRST OPERATOR *rising, to* CAROLINE) Is
that ready yet, Miss?

CAROLINE. (*rising, hesitating, getting* L. *of and a
little above table* R. C.) Yes, but I—(*finally starts to
hand it up to him*) Of course you've—(*hesitates*)
You've got to take it!

FIRST OPERATOR. (*near* CAROLINE *on her* R. *A
brief puzzled look at her*) Yes, of course.

(*She hands him the dispatch. He at once opens it.*)

CAROLINE. (*sharp scream*) Oh! (*quickly seizes
the paper out of his hand. They stand looking at
one another a little* L. *of and above table* R. C.) Ah
didn't tell you to *read* it!

FIRST OPERATOR. (*after look at her*) What did
you want?

CAROLINE. Ah want you to *send* it!

FIRST OPERATOR. How am I going to send it if I
don't read it?

CAROLINE. (*after looking at him in consternation*) Do—you—mean—to—say—

FIRST OPERATOR. I've got to spell out every word!
Didn't you know that?

CAROLINE. (*sadly, and shaking her head from side
to side*) Oh—Ah must have—but Ah— (CAROLINE
pauses trying to think what to do)

FIRST OPERATOR. Would there be any harm in
my——

CAROLINE. (*turning on him with sudden vehemence*) Why Ah wouldn't have you see it for worlds!
My gracious! (*she soon opens the dispatch and looks
at it*)

FIRST OPERATOR. (*good-naturedly*) Is it as bad
as all that!

CAROLINE. Bad! It isn't bad at all! On'y—Ah
only don't want it to get out all over the town—
that's all!

FIRST OPERATOR. It won't ever get out from this
office, Miss. (CAROLINE *looks steadfastly at* FIRST
OPERATOR) We wouldn't be allowed to mention
anything outside!

CAROLINE. (*a doubtful look at him*) You
wouldn't!

FIRST OPERATOR. No Miss. All sorts of private
stuff goes through here.

CAROLINE. (*with new hope*) Does it?

FIRST OPERATOR. Every day! Now if that's anything important——

CAROLINE. (*impulsively*) O yes—it's— (*recovering herself*)—it is!

FIRST OPERATOR. Then I reckon you'd better trust
it to me.

(CAROLINE *looks at* OPERATOR *a moment.*)

CAROLINE. Ye—yes—Ah reckon Ah had! (*she
hesitatingly hands him her telegram*)

(FIRST OPERATOR *takes the paper and at once turns*

away to the table R. *as if to go to business of
sending it on instrument* B.)

CAROLINE. (*quickly*) Oh stop! (FIRST OPERA-
TOR *turns and looks at her from table down* R.) Wait
till I— (*going up stage toward door hurriedly*)
Ah don't want to be here—while you *spell out every
word!* Ah couldn't stand *that!*

(FIRST OPERATOR *stands good-naturedly waiting.*
   CAROLINE *takes hold of* MARTHA *to start out of
   door with her. Enter* EDDINGER—*a private in
   a gray uniform—at door up* R. CAROLINE *and*
   MARTHA *stand back out of his way. He glances
   at them and at once goes down to* FIRST OPERA-
   TOR *on his* L., *salutes and hands him a written
   order and crosses in front of table* R. C. *to*
   L. C., *wheels and stands at attention facing* R.
   FIRST OPERATOR *looks at the order, glances at*
   EDDINGER, *then at* CAROLINE. CAROLINE *and*
   MARTHA *move as if to go out at door up* R.)

FIRST OPERATOR. Wait a minute, please! (*stand-
ing near table down* R. CAROLINE *and* MARTHA *stop
and turn toward* FIRST OPERATOR) Are you Miss
Mitford?
   CAROLINE. Yes—Ah'm Miss Mitford!
   FIRST OPERATOR. I don't understand this! Here's
an order just come in to hold back any dispatch you
give us.
   CAROLINE. (*after looking speechless at* FIRST
OPERATOR *a moment*) Hold back any—hold back—
   FIRST OPERATOR. Yes Miss. And that ain't the
worst of it!
   CAROLINE. Wh—what else is there? (*comes
down* C. *a little way looking at* FIRST OPERATOR *with
wide open eyes.* MARTHA *remains up near door up*
R.)

FIRST OPERATOR. (R.) This man has orders to take it back with him. (*slight pause*)

CAROLINE. (C.) Take it back with him? Take what back with him?

FIRST OPERATOR. (*near table down R.*) Your dispatch Miss. (CAROLINE *simply opens mouth and slowly draws in her breath*) There must be some mistake, but that's what the order says.

CAROLINE. (*with unnatural calmness*) And where does it say to take it back to?

FIRST OPERATOR. (*looks at the order*) The name is Arrelsford! (*brief pause*)

CAROLINE. The order is for that man— (*indicating* EDDINGER L. C.) to take my dispatch back to Mr. Arrelsford?

FIRST OPERATOR. Yes Miss.

CAROLINE. An' does it say anything in there about what Ah'm goin' to be doin' in the meantime?

FIRST OPERATOR. No.

CAROLINE. That's too bad!

FIRST OPERATOR. I'm right sorry this has occurred Miss, and— (*interrupted*)

CAROLINE. Oh—(*shaking head*) there isn't any occasion for your feeling sorry—because it hasn't occurred! And besides that it isn't goin' to occur! (*becoming excited*) When it does you can go aroun' bein' sorry all you like! Have you got the faintest idea that Ah'm goin' to let him take my telegram away with him and show it to that man! Do you suppose——

MARTHA. (*coming forward a step from up R. C. near the door. Breaking in in a voice like a siren*) No, sir! You ain't a goin' ter do it—you can be right sure you ain't!

FIRST OPERATOR. (R.) But what can I do, Miss?

CAROLINE. (C. *advancing*) You can either send it or hand it back to me—that's what you can do!

MARTHA. (*calling out from up* R. C.) Yes suh—that's the very best thing you can do! An' the sooner you do it the quicker it'll be done—Ah kin tell you that right now!

FIRST OPERATOR. But this man has come here with orders to——

CAROLINE. (*going defiantly to* EDDINGER *and facing him*) Well this man can go straight back and report to Mr. Arrelsford that he was unable to carry out his orders! (*defiant attitude toward* ED-DINGER L. C.) That's what he can do!

MARTHA. (*from up* R. C.—*now thoroughly roused and coming to a sense of her responsibility*) Let 'im take it! Let 'im take it ef he wants to so pow'fle bad! Just let the other one there give it to him—an' then see 'im try an' git out through this do' with it! (*standing solidly before door up* R. C. *with folded arms and ominously shaking head.* MARTHA *talks and mumbles on half to herself*) Ah want to see him go by! Ah'm just a' waitin' fur a sight o' him gittin' past dis do'! That's what ah'm waitin' fur! (*goes on talking half to herself, quieting down grad-ually*) Ah'd like to know what they s'pose it was Ah comeda round yere for anyway—these men with their orders an' fussin' an'——

FIRST OPERATOR. (*down* R. *when quiet is restored*) Miss Mitford, if I was to give this dispatch back to you now it would get me into a heap o' trouble.

CAROLINE. (C. *looking at him*) What kind of trouble?

FIRST OPERATOR. (R.) Might be put in prison—might be shot!

CAROLINE. You mean they might——

FIRST OPERATOR. Sure to do one or the other!

CAROLINE. Just for givin' it back to me?

FIRST OPERATOR. That's all.

CAROLINE. (*after looking silently at* FIRST OPERA-TOR *a moment*) Then you'll have to keep it!

FIRST OPERATOR. (*after slight pause, sincerely*) Thank you Miss Mitford!

CAROLINE. (*a sigh—reconciling herself to the situation*) Very well—that's understood! You don't give it back to me—an' you can't give it to him—so nobody's disobeying any orders at all! (*going up and getting a chair from up o. and bringing it forward*) And that's the way it stands! (*banging chair down to emphasize her words close to* EDDINGER *and directly between him and the* FIRST OPERATOR, *then plumps herself down on the chair and facing* R., *looks unconcerned*) Ah reckon Ah can stay as long as he can! (*half to herself*) Ah haven't got much to do!

FIRST OPERATOR. But Miss Mitford——

CAROLINE. Now there ain't any good o' talkin'! If you've got any telegraphin' to do you better do it. Ah won't disturb you!

(*Rapid steps heard in corridor outside up* R. *Enter* MR. ARRELSFORD *door up* R. *coming in hurriedly, somewhat flushed and excited. He looks hastily about, and goes at once down* R. O. *toward* FIRST OPERATOR.)

ARRELSFORD. (R. O.) What's this! Didn't he get here in time?

FIRST OPERATOR. (R.) Are you Mr. Arrelsford?

ARRELSFORD. Yes. (*sharp glance at* CAROLINE) Are you holding back a dispatch?

FIRST OPERATOR. Yes sir.

ARRELSFORD. Why didn't he bring it?

FIRST OPERATOR. Well, Miss Mitford—(*hesitates, with a motion toward* CAROLINE)

ARRELSFORD. (*comprehending*) Oh! (*crosses back of* CAROLINE *and* EDDINGER *to* L.) Eddinger! (EDDINGER *wheels to* L. *facing him*) Report back to Corporal Matson. Tell him to send a surgeon to the prisoner who was wounded at General Varney's house—if he isn't dead by this time! (*moves over to* L. *as* EDDINGER *goes up.* CAROLINE *turns and looks at* ARRELSFORD *on hearing cue " prisoner," rising at same time and pushing chair back up* C. EDDINGER *salutes and exits quickly up* R. C., *going back of* CAROLINE. ARRELSFORD *turns and starts toward* FIRST OPERATOR) Let me see what that dispatch—

(FIRST OPERATOR *stands* R. *with* CAROLINE'S *dispatch in his hand.* CAROLINE *steps quickly in front of* ARRELSFORD. ARRELSFOTD *stops in some surprise at* CAROLINE'S *sudden move.*)

CAROLINE. (*facing* ARRELSFORD) Ah expect you think you're going to get my telegram an' read it?

ARRELSFORD. (L. C.) I certainly intend to do so!

CAROLINE. (C.) Well there's a great big disappointment loomin' up right in front of you!

ARRELSFORD. (*with suspicion*) So! You've been trying to send out something you don't want us to see!

CAROLINE. What if Ah have?

ARRELSFORD. Just this! You won't send it—and I'll see it! (*about to pass* CAROLINE) This is a case where— (CAROLINE *steps in front of* ARRELSFORD *again so that he has to stop*)

CAROLINE. This is a case where you ain't goin' to read my private writin' (*stands looking at him with blazing eyes*)

ARRELSFORD. Lieutenant—I have an order here putting me in charge! Bring that dispatch to me!

(FIRST OPERATOR *about to move toward* ARRELSFORD *with the dispatch.* MARTHA *suddenly steps down in front of* FIRST OPERATOR *with ponderous tread and stands facing him.*)

MARTHA. (R. C.) Mistah Lieutenant can stay juss about whar he is! (*brief pause*)

ARRELSFORD. (L. *to* FIRST OPERATOR) Is that Miss Mitford's dispatch?

FIRST OPERATOR. (R.) Yes sir!

ARRELSFORD. Read it! (CAROLINE *turns with a gasp of horror.* MARTHA *turns in slow anger.* FIRST OPERATOR *stands surprised for an instant*) Read it out!

CAROLINE. You shan't do such a thing! You have no right to read a private telegram—(etc.)

MARTHA. (*speaking with* CAROLINE) No sah! He ain't no business to read her letters—none whatsomever! (etc.)

ARRELSFORD. (*angrily*) Silence! (CAROLINE *and* MARTHA *stop talking*) If you interfere any further with the business of this office I'll have you both put under arrest! *to* FIRST OPERATOR) Read that dispatch!

(CAROLINE *gasps breathless at* ARRELSFORD—*then turns and buries her face on* MARTHA's *shoulder sobbing.*)

FIRST OPERATOR. (*reads with some difficulty*) " forgive me—Wilfred darling—please—forgive me and I will help you all I can."

ARRELSFORD. That dispatch can't go! (*turns and moves left a few steps*)

CAROLINE. (*turning and facing* ARRELSFORD. *Almost calm with anger*) That dispatch can go! An' that dispatch will go! (ARRELSFORD *turns and looks at* CAROLINE *from* L. MARTHA *moves up on right side ready to exit, standing well up* C. *and turning toward* ARRELSFORD) Ah know someone whose orders even you are bound to respect and someone who'll come here with me an' see that you do it!

ARRELSFORD. (L.) I can show good and sufficient reasons for what I do!

CAROLINE. (C.) Well you'll have to show good and sufficienter reasons than you've shown to me—Ah can tell you that, Mr. Arrelsford!

ARRELSFORD. I give my reasons to my superiors, Miss Mitford!

CAROLINE. Then you'll have to go 'round givin' 'em to everybody in Richmond, Mr. Arrelsford! (*saying which* CAROLINE *makes a deep courtesy and turns and sweeps out through door up* R. *followed in the same spirit by* MARTHA *who turns at the door and also makes a profound courtesy to* ARRELSFORD, *going off haughtily*)

(FIRST OPERATOR *sits down at table* R. C. *and begins to write.* ARRELSFORD *looks after* CAROLINE *an instant and then goes rapidly over to* FIRST OPERATOR.)

ARRELSFORD. Let me see that dispatch!

FIRST OPERATOR. (*slight doubt*) You said you had an order, sir.

ARRELSFORD. (*impatiently*) Yes—yes! (*throws order down on telegraph table*) Don't waste time!

(FIRST OPERATOR *picks up order and looks closely at it for an instant.*)

FIRST OPERATOR. Department order sir?

ARRELSFORD. (*assenting shortly*) Yes.

FIRST OPERATOR. I suppose you're Mr. Arrelsford all right?

ARRELSFORD. Of course!

FIRST OPERATOR. We have to be pretty careful sir! (*hands him* CAROLINE'S *telegram and goes on writing.* ARRELSFORD *takes* CAROLINE'S *telegram eagerly and reads it. Thinks an instant. Going toward* L. *to* C. *turns to* FIRST OPERATOR)

ARRELSFORD. (C.) Did she seem nervous or excited when she handed this in?

FIRST OPERATOR. *(at table* R. C.) She certainly did!

ARRELSFORD. Anxious not to have it seen?

FIRST OPERATOR. Anxious! I should say so! She didn't want me to see it!

ARRELSFORD. We've got a case on here and she's mixed up in it!

FIRST OPERATOR. But that dispatch is to young Varney—the General's son!

ARRELSFORD. *(shortly)* So much the worse! It's one of the ugliest affairs we ever had! I had them put me on it and I've got it down pretty close! *(going across to* L. C.) We'll end it right here in this office inside of thirty minutes!

(Enter a PRIVATE *at door up* R. *He comes down at once to* ARRELSFORD.)

ARRELSFORD. (L. C. *turning to* PRIVATE) Well, what is it?

PRIVATE. (L. C. R. *of* ARRELSFORD. *Reporting)* The lady's here sir!

ARRELSFORD. Where is she?

PRIVATE. Waiting down below—at the front entrance.

ARRELSFORD. Did she come alone?

PRIVATE. Yes sir.

ARRELSFORD. Show her the way up. (PRIVATE *salutes and exits at door up* R. ARRELSFORD *comes* C. *to* FIRST OPERATOR) I suppose you've got a revolver there? (FIRST OPERATOR *brings up revolver in matter-of-fact way from beneath his table and puts it on table, resuming business of writing, etc.)* I'd rather handle this thing myself—but I might call on you. Be ready—that's all!

FIRST OPERATOR. Yes sir.

ARRELSFORD. Obey any orders you get an' send out all dispatches unless I stop you.

FIRST OPERATOR. Very well sir.

(*Door up* R. *is opening by the* PRIVATE *last on, and*
     EDITH *is shown in.* ARRELSFORD *meets her.*
     The PRIVATE *exits at door up* R.)

EDITH. (C. *pretty well up, in a low voice*) I—
I've accepted your invitation!

ARRELSFORD. (*up* C. *on* EDITH'S L.) I'm greatly
obliged Miss Varney! As a matter of justice to me
it was— (FIRST OPERATOR *puts revolver back on
shelf under table* L. C.)

EDITH. (*interrupting*) I didn't come to oblige
you! I'm here to see that no more—(*pause*) mur-
ders are committed in order to satisfy your singular
curiosity.

ARRELSFORD. (*looks at her an instant. She at him*)

ARRELSFORD. (*after brief pause*) Is the man
dead?

EDITH. (*looking at* ARRELSFORD *steadily*) The
man is dead. (*short pause*)

ARRELSFORD. (*going down* L. C. *a little turns to
her. With cutting emphasis but low voice—so as not
to be overheard*) It's a curious thing, Miss Varney,
that a Yankee prisoner more or less should make so
much difference to you. They're dying down in
Libby by the hundreds!

EDITH. At least they're not killed in our houses—
before our very eyes!

(*Enter an* ORDERLY *who is a Special Agent of the
     War Department at door up* R. *He comes
     quickly in and crosses to* ARRELSFORD L. C. *then
     glances round toward* FIRST OPERATOR. ARRELS-
     FORD *moves down stage to speak to the* ORDERLY.
     EDITH *remains up* C.)

ARRELSFORD. (L. *low voice*) Well, have you kept
track of him?

ORDERLY. (L. C. *low voice*)   He's coming up Fourth Street, sir!

ARRELSFORD. (*low voice*)   Where has he been?

ORDERLY. (*low voice*)   To his quarters on Cary Street. We got in the next room and watched him through a transom.

ARRELSFORD. (*low voice*)   What was he doing?

ORDERLY. (*low voice*)   Working at some papers or documents.

ARRELSFORD. (*low voice*)   Could you see them? Could you see what it was?

ORDERLY. (*low voice*)   Headings looked like orders from the War Department.

ARRELSFORD. (*low voice*)   He's coming in here with forged orders!

ORDERLY. (*low voice*)   Yes sir.

ARRELSFORD. (*low voice*)   His game is to get control of these wires and then send out dispatches to the front that'll take away a battery from some vital point!

ORDERLY. (*low voice*)   Looks like it sir.

ARRELSFORD. (*low voice*)   And that vital point is what the Yankees mean by Plan Three! That's where they'll hit us. (*glances round quickly considering—goes up* L. *to above line of middle window— turns to* ORDERLY)   Is there a guard in this building?

ORDERLY. (*going up near* ARRELSFORD *on his* R. *low voice*)   Not inside—there's a guard in front and sentries around the barracks over in the square.

ARRELSFORD. (*low voice*)   They could hear me from this window, couldn't they?

ORDERLY. (*low voice*)   The guard could hear you. (*a glance toward door* R.)   He must be nearly here sir, you'd better look out!

EDITH. (*up* C. *low voice*)   Where shall I go?

ARRELSFORD. (*up* L. *low voice*)   Outside here— on the balcony—I'll be with you!

EDITH. (*low voice*) But—if he comes to the window!

ARRELSFORD. (*low voice*) We'll step in at the next one. (*to* ORDERLY) See if the window of the Commissary-General's office is open.

(ORDERLY *crosses* ARRELSFORD *and steps quickly out of window up* L. *through middle window, and goes off along balcony to* L. *He returns at once re-entering through middle window.*)

ORDERLY. The next window's open sir.

ARRELSFORD. That's all I want of you—report back to Corporal Matson. Tell him to get the body of that prisoner out of the Varney house—he knows where it's to go!

ORDERLY. Very well sir! (*salutes, crosses and exits door up* R.)

ARRELSFORD. (*to* EDITH) This way please! (*conducts* EDITH *out through middle window to the balcony up* L. *She exits to* L. ARRELSFORD *is closing the window to follow when he sees a* MESSENGER *enter up* R. *and thereupon he stops just in the window keeping out of sight behind window frame*)

(*Enter* MESSENGER 1 *at door up* R. C. *He takes his position up stage waiting for messages as before.* ARRELSFORD *eyes him sharply an instant—then comes forward a step.*)

ARRELSFORD. (*from window up* L.) Where did you come from?

MESSENGER 1. (*up* C.) War Department sir.

ARRELSFORD. Carrying dispatches?

MESSENGER 1. Yes sir.

ARRELSFORD. You know me don't you?

MESSENGER 1. I've seen you at the office sir.

ARRELSFORD. I'm here on Department business.
All you've got to do is to keep quiet about it! (*Exit*
ARRELSFORD *at middle window up* L. *which he closes
after him and then disappears from view along
balcony to* L. MESSENGER 1 *moves well over up* L.)

(*Enter* MESSENGER 2 *at door up* R. C. *He takes his
place at up* L. *with* MESSENGER 1. FIRST OPER-
ATOR *busy at table* R. C. *Moment's wait. Enter*
CAPTAIN THORNE *at door up* R. C. *As he comes
down he gives one quick glance about the room
and to* L. *but almost instantly to front again, so
that it would hardly be noticed. He wears cap
and carries an order in his belt.* THORNE *goes
down at once to* L. *of table* R. C. *and faces* FIRST
OPERATOR.)

THORNE. (*saluting*) Lieutenant! (*hands* FIRST
OPERATOR *the order which he carried in his belt.*)

(FIRST OPERATOR *turns, sees* THORNE, *rises, saluting
briefly, takes the order, opens and looks at it.*)

FIRST OPERATOR. Order from the Department.
(*moves* R. *a little to give* THORNE *chance to get to
back of table*)
THORNE. (*motionless, facing to* R.) I believe so.
(*quickly glances at door up* R. *as* OPERATOR *is looking at the order*)
FIRST OPERATOR. They want me to take a cipher
dispatch ovah to the President's house.
THORNE. (*moving to take* FIRST OPERATOR'S
*place at table—pulls chair back a little and then
tosses cap over on table* R.) Yes—I'm ordered on
here till you get back. (*goes to place back of table*
R. C. *and stands arranging things on the table*)
FIRST OPERATOR. (*at table* R. *looking front or
to* R. *a little*) That's an odd thing. They told me

the President was down here with the Cabinet! He must have just now gone home I reckon.

THORNE. (*standing at table* R. C. *and arranging papers, etc. on it*) Looks like it.—If he isn't there you'd better wait. (*looking through a bunch of dispatches as he speaks above*)

FIRST OPERATOR. (*gets his cap from table* R. *puts it on. At table* R.) Yes—I'll wait! (*pause*) You'll have to look out for Allison's wires, Cap'n. He was called ovah to the Department.

(THORNE *stops and looks front an instant on mention of* ALLISON.)

THORNE. (*easy manner again*) Ah ha—Allison!

FIRST OPERATOR. Yes.

THORNE. . Be gone long? (THORNE *business of throwing used sheets in waste-basket and fixing a couple of large envelopes ready for quick use*)

FIRST OPERATOR. Well, you know how it is— they generally whip around quite a while before they make up their minds what they want to do. I don't expect they'll trouble you much! It's as quiet as a church down the river. (*starting up toward door up* R.)

THORNE. (*seeing a cigar on the table near instrument*) See here—wait a minute—you'd better not walk out and leave a—no matter! (FIRST OPERATOR *stops and turns back to* THORNE—*comes* C. *a little*) It's none of my business. (*tapping with the end of a long envelope on table where the cigar is*) Still, if you want some good advice, that's a dangerous thing to do!

FIRST OPERATOR. (*coming down*) What is it Cap'n?

THORNE. Leave a cigar lying around this office like that! (*picks it up with* L. *hand and lights a match with* R.) Somebody might walk in here any minute and take it away! (*about to light cigar*) I can't watch your cigars all day (*lighting cigar*)

FIRST OPERATOR. (*laughing*) Oh! Help yourself Cap'n!

THORNE. (*suddenly snatching cigar out of mouth with* L. *hand and looking at it*) What's the matter with it? Oh well—I'll take a chance. (*puts it in his mouth and resumes lighting*)

(FIRST OPERATOR *hesitates a moment, then goes down near* THORNE *on his* L., L. *of table* R. C.)

FIRST OPERATOR. (*a little above* THORNE, *confidentially*) Cap'n, if there's any trouble around here you'll find a revolver under there. (*indicating shelf under table.* THORNE *stops lighting cigar an instant. Eyes motionless front. Match blazes up*)

THORNE. (*at once resuming nonchalance—finishing lighting cigar*) What about that? What makes you think—(*pulling in to light cigar*) there's going to be trouble?

FIRST OPERATOR. Oh well, there might be!

THORNE. (*tossing match away*) Been having a dream?

FIRST OPERATOR. Oh no—but you never can tell! (*starts up* R. *toward door*)

THORNE. (*cigar in mouth. Going at papers again*) That's right! You never can tell. But see here—hold on a minute! (*reaching down and getting revolver from shelf and tossing it on table near* L. *end*) If you never can tell you'd better take that along with you. I've got one of my own. (*rather sotto voce*) I *can* tell!

(*Click of instrument* A. THORNE *answers on instrument* A. *at* R. *end of table* R. C. *and slides into chair.*)

FIRST OPERATOR. Well, if you've got one here, I might as well. (*takes revolver*) Look out for yourself, Cap'n! (*goes up. Instrument A. begins clicking off a message.* THORNE *sits at table R. C. listening and ready to take down what comes*)

THORNE. (*listening to instrument at R.*) Same to you old man—and many happy returns of the day! (*Exit* FIRST OPERATOR *door up R. C.* THORNE *writes message, briefly addresses long envelope. Instrument A. stops receiving as* THORNE *addresses envelope.* THORNE *O. K.'s dispatch*) Ready here! MESSENGER 1 *down to* THORNE *and salutes L. of table R. C.*) Quartermaster-General. (*handing dispatch to* MESSENGER)

MESSENGER 1. Not at his office, sir!

THORNE. Find him! He's got to have it!

MESSENGER 1. Very well sir! (*salutes. Exits quickly up R.*)

(THORNE *turns slowly L. looking to see if there is a* MESSENGER *there. Sees there is one without looking entirely around. A second's wait. Instrument C. upper end of table R. begins to click.* THORNE *quickly rises and going to instrument C. answers call—on instrument—drops into chair up R. and writes message—puts it in envelope. O. K.'s call.*)

THORNE. Ready here! (MESSENGER 2 *goes quickly across to* THORNE L. *of table R. and salutes*) Secretary of the Treasury—marked private. Take it to his house. (*begins to read a dispatch he twitched off from a file*)

MESSENGER 2. He's down yere at the cabinet, sir.

THORNE. Take it to his house and wait till he comes!

(MESSENGER 2 *salutes and exits door up R. C. closing the door after him. On the slam of door after*

MESSENGER 2 THORNE *crushes dispatch in* R.
*hand and throws it to floor—and wheels front
—his eyes on the instrument down* R. C. *All
one quick movement. Then he rises and with
cat-like swiftness springs to the door up* R.
*and listens—opens the door a little and looks
off. Closes it quickly, turning swiftly to* C.
and opens the door up C. *glancing in. Then
goes to the window up* L. C.—*the nearest.
Pushes it open a little and looks off through
window and begins at same time to unbuckle
belt and unbutton coat. Turns and moves
down toward the telegraph table* R. C. *at same
time throwing belt over to* R. *above* R. *table,
and taking off coat. Glances back up* L.—*looks
to see that a document is in breast pocket of
coat—letting audience see that it is there—and
lays coat over back of chair above table* R. C. *with
document in sight so that he can get it without
delay. Takes revolver from hip pocket and
quickly but quietly lays it on the table* R. C. *just
to right of the instrument and then seizes key of
instrument* A. *and gives a certain call;
(—.... .. ..) Waits. A glance rapidly to
left. He is standing at table—cigar in mouth.
Makes the call again:* (—.... .. ..) *Waits
again. Gives the call third time:* (— ....
..) *Goes to lower end of table* R. *and half
sits on it, folding arms, eyes on instrument,
chewing cigar, with a glance or two up stage, but
his eyes come quickly back to the instrument.
Slides off table—takes cigar out of his mouth
with* L. *hand and gives the call again with right:*
(—.... .. ..) *putting cigar in mouth again
and turning and walking up stage looking
about. Soon he carelessly throws papers which
he took from* R. *pocket—off up stage. Just as
he throws papers—facing to* L.—*the call is*

answered: (—.... .. ..) THORNE *is back
at the table* R. C. *in an instant and telegraphing rapidly—cigar in mouth. When he has
sent for about five seconds steps are heard
in corridor outside up* R. THORNE *quickly strikes
a match—which is close at hand to* R. *of instrument—and sinks into the chair, appearing to be
lazily lighting his cigar as a* MESSENGER *comes
in at door up* R. C. MESSENGER 4 *enters as soon
as he hears match strike at door up* R. C.—*He
goes down at once to* THORNE *with dispatch.
Salutes and extends it toward* THORNE—*on*
THORNE'S *left.*)

MESSENGER 4.   Secretary of War, Cap'n!   Wants
to go out right now!   (THORNE *tosses away match,
takes dispatch and opens it.* MESSENGER 4 *salutes,
turns and starts up toward door*)

THORNE.   Here!   Here!   What's all this!   (*looking at the dispatch.* MESSENGER 4 *returns to*
THORNE—*salutes*)   Is that the Secretary's signature?

MESSENGER 4.   Yes sir—I saw him sign it.

(THORNE *looks closely at the signature. Turns it so
as to get gas light. Turns and looks sharply at
the* MESSENGER. *Back to dispatch again. Puts
it on table and writes an* O. K. *on it.*)

THORNE.   (*writing*)   Um hm—saw him sign it
did you?

MESSENGER 4.   Yes sir.

THORNE.   (*writing*)   Got to be a little careful to-
night!   (*holding dispatch up from table in* L. *hand,
so that audience can see it is the same one—with the
Secretary's signature*)

MESSENGER 4.   I can swear to that one, sir.
(*salutes—turns and goes up and exits at door up* R.)

(THORNE *listens—faced front for exit of* MESSENGER. *Dispatch in* L. *hand. Instantly on slam of door up* L C. *he puts cigar down at end of table, rises, laying the dispatch down flat on table. Quickly folds and very dexterously and rapidly cuts off the lower part of the paper which has the signature of the Secretary of War upon it, holds it between his teeth and tears the rest of the order in pieces, which he is on the point of throwing into waste-basket at* L. *of table when he stops and changes his mind, stuffing the torn-up dispatch into his* R. *hand trousers pocket. Picks up coat from back of chair and takes the document out of inside breast pocket. Opens it out on table and quickly pastes to it the piece of the real order bearing the signature, wipes quickly with handkerchief, puts handkerchief back into pocket, picks up cigar which he laid down on table and puts it in mouth, at same time sitting and at once beginning to telegraph rapidly on instrument* A. *rapid click of the instrument.* THORNE *intent, yet vigilant. During business of* THORNE *pasting dispatch,* ARRELSFORD *appears outside windows up* L. *at side of columns. He motions off toward* L. EDITH *comes into view there also.* ARRELSFORD *points toward* THORNE, *calling her attention to what he is doing. They stand at the window watching* THORNE—*the strong moonlight bringing them out sharply. After a few seconds* AR- RELSFORD *accidentally makes a slight noise with latch of window. Instantly on this faint click of latch* THORNE *stops telegraphing and sits absolutely motionless—his eyes front.—*ARRELSFORD *and* EDITH *exit quickly and noiselessly on balcony to* L. *Dead silence. After a motionless pause,* THORNE'S *hand very quietly glides from the telegraph instrument to the revolver—*

which is just to right of it, and raising L. *hand to cigar to twist it or some movement to cover bus. he slides revolver off table at* R. *and gets it down on his* R. *side. He then begins to push things about on the table with* L. *hand as if looking for something and soon rises as if not able to find it, and looking still more carefully.* THORNE *keeps revolver close against* R. *side—looks about on table, glances over to table on* R. *as if looking for what he wanted there, puts cigar down on table before him—after about to do so once and taking a final puff—and steps over to table at* R. *still looking for something, and keeping revolver out of sight of anyone at window up* L. *As he looks he raises* L. *hand carelessly to the cock of the gas bracket and instantly shuts off light. Stage dark. Instantly on lights off,* THORNE *drops on one knee behind —that is to* R. *of table* R. C.*—facing toward* L. *Revolver covering up* L. *Light from windows up* L. C. *gauged to strike across to* THORNE *at table with revolver. After holding it a short time, he begins slowly to edge up stage—holding to chair-backs at* R. *He then edges cautiously up on* R. *until within reach of the door, when he suddenly slides the heavy bolt, thus locking the doors on the inside. From doors up* R. THORNE *glides with a dash—throwing aside the chair in the way—at the door of closet up* C. *which opens down stage and hinges on its* L. *side. With motion of reaching it he has it open—if not already open—and pushing it along before him as he moves left toward window. When moving slowly behind this door with is eyes and revolver on window the telegraph instrument down* R. C. *suddenly gives two or three sharp clicks.* THORNE *makes an instantaneous turn front covering the instrument with revolver.*

Sees what it was. Turns L. *again. Just as he gets door nearly wide open against wall at back he dashes at windows up* L. C. *and bangs them open with* L. *hand covering all outside with revolver in his* R. *In an instant sees that no one is there. Straightens up—looking. Quick spring past first window stopping close behind the upright between first and second windows, and at same time banging these windows open and covering with revolver. Sees no one. Looks this way and that. Makes quick dash outside and covers over balustrade—as if someone might be below. In again quick. Looks about with one or two quick glances. Concludes he must have been mistaken, and starts down toward table* R. C.—*stops after going two or three steps and looks back. Turns and goes rapidly down to table. Picks up cigar with* L. *hand. Puts revolver at* R. *end of table with* R. *hand, and gets a match with that hand. Stands an instant looking* L. *Strikes match and is about to relight cigar. Pause—eyes front. Match burning. Listening. Looks* L.—*lights cigar—as he is lighting cigar thinks of gas being out, and steps to right, turns it on and lights it. Lights full on.* THORNE *turns quickly, looking left as lights on. Then steps at once—after glancing quickly about room—to telegraph table, puts down cigar near upper* R. *corner of table with* L. *hand and begins to telegraph with* L. *hand, facing front. Suddenly sharp report of revolver outside through lower window, up* L. *with crash of glass and on it* ARRELSFORD *springs on at middle window* L. *with revolver in his hand.* THORNE *does not move on shot except quick recoil from instrument, leaning back a little, expression of pain an instant. His* L. *hand— with which he was telegraphing—is covered with*

*blood. He stands motionless an instant. Eyes
then down toward his own revolver. Slight
pause. He makes a sudden plunge for it getting
it in his* R. *hand. At same instant quick turn
on* ARRELSFORD *but before he can raise the
weapon* ARRELSFORD *covers him with revolver
and* THORNE *stops where he is, holding position.*)

ARRELSFORD. (L. C. *covering* THORNE) Drop it!
(*pause*) Drop that gun or you're a dead man! Drop
it I say! (*a moment's pause.* THORNE *gradually
recovers to erect position again, looking easily front,
and puts revolver on the table, picking up cigar with
same hand and putting it casually into his mouth as
if he thought he'd have a smoke after all, instead of
killing a man. He then gets handkerchief out of
pocket with* R. *hand and gets hold of a corner of it·
not using his* L. ARRELSFORD *advances a step or two,
lowering revolver, but holding it ready*) ·Do you
know why I didn't kill you like a dog just now?

THORNE. (*back of table* R. C. *as he twists handkerchief around his wounded hand*) Because you're
such a damn bad shot.

ARRELSFORD. Maybe you'll change your mind
about that!

THORNE. (*arranging handkerchief to cover his
wounded hand—leaving fingers free. Speaks easily
and pleasantly*) Well I hope so I'm sure. It isn't
pleasant to be riddled up this way you know!

ARRELSFORD. Next time you'll be riddled some·
where else besides the hand! There's only one reason why you're not lying there now with a bullet
through your head!

THORNE. Only one, eh?

ARRELSFORD. Only one!

THORNE. (*still fixing hand and sleeve*) Do I
hear it?

ARRELSFORD. Simply because I gave my word of

honor to someone outside there that I wouldn't kill
you now!

(THORNE *on hearing " Someone outside there " turns
and looks at* ARRELSFORD *with interest.*)

THORNE. (*taking cigar out of mouth and holding
it in* R. *hand as he moves toward* ARRELSFORD) Ah!
Then it isn't a litle tete-a-tete between ourselves!
You have someone with you! (*stopping near* C.
coolly facing ARRELSFORD)

ARRELSFORD. (*sarcastically*) I *have* someone with
me Captain Thorne! Someone who takes quite an
interest in what you're doing to-night!

THORNE. (*puts cigar in mouth*) Quite an interest, eh! That's kind I'm sure. (*takes cigar out of
mouth facing front*) Is the gentleman going to stay
out there all alone on the cold balcony, or shall I
have the pleasure—(*enter* EDITH *from balcony up
L. through the upper window, where she stands supporting herself by the sides. She is looking toward
R. as if intending to go, but not able for a moment,
to move. Avoids looking at* THORNE)—of inviting
him in here and having a charming little three-
handed—(*glancing up toward window he sees* EDITH
*and stops motionless. Looks at her quietly a moment
—then turns slowly and looks at* ARRELSFORD—*who
has a slight smile on his lips; then turns front and
holds position motionless*)

EDITH. (*does not speak until after* THORNE *looks
front. Low voice*) I'll go, Mr. Arrelsford!

ARRELSFORD. Not yet, Miss Varney!

EDITH. (*coming blindly into the room a few steps
as if to get across to the door up* R.) I don't wish
to stay—any longer!

ARRELSFORD. (*down* L. C.) One moment please!
We need you!

(EDITH *stops.*)

EDITH. (*up* C.) For what?

ARRELSFORD. A witness.

EDITH. You can send for me. I'll be at home. (*about to start toward door*)

ARRELSFORD. (*sharply*) I'll have to detain you till I turn him over to the guard—it won't take a moment! (*steps to the middle window, still keeping an eye on* THORNE, *and calls off in loud voice*) Corporal o' the guard! Corporal o' the guard! Send up the guard will you!

(EDITH *shrinks back up* C. *not knowing what to do.*)

VOICE. (*outside up* L. *in distance—as if down below in the street. Be sure to get distance for this or it will be ruined*) What's the matter up there! Who's calling the guard!

ARRELSFORD. (*at window*) Up here! Department Telegraph! Send 'em up quick!

VOICES. (*outside distant as before*) Corporal of the Guard Post Four! (*repeated more distant*) Corporal of the Guard Post Four! (*repeated again almost inaudible*) Corporal of the Guard Post Four! Fall in the guard! Fall in! (*these orders gruff—indistinct—distant. Give effect of quick gruff shouts of orders barely audibly*)

EDITH. (*up* C. *turning suddenly upon* ARRELSFORD) I'm not going to stay! I don't wish to be a witness!

ARRELSFORD. (L. C. *after an instant's look at* EDITH—*suspecting the reason for her refusal*) Whatever your feelings may be Miss Varney, we can't permit you to refuse!

EDITH. (*with determination*) I do refuse! If you won't take me down to the street I'll find the way out myself! (*stops as she is turning to go, on hearing the* GUARD *outside*)

(*Sound of* GUARD *running through lower corridors.*

tramp of men coming up stairway and along hallways outside up R. THORNE *holds position looking steadily front, cigar in* R. *hand.*)

ARRELSFORD. (*loud voice to stop* EDITH) Too late! The guard is here! (*steps down* L. C. *with revolver, his eyes on* THORNE)

(EDITH *stands an instant and then as the* GUARD *is heard nearer in the corridor up* R. *she moves up to window up* L. *and remains there until sound of* GUARD *breaking in the door. Then she makes her exit off to* L. *on balcony. Disappearing so as to attract no attention.*)

ARRELSFORD. (*shouting across to* THORNE) I've got you about where I want you at last! (THORNE *motionless. Sound of hurried tread of men outside up* R. *as if coming on double quick toward the door, on bare floor of corridor*) You thought you was almighty smart—but you'll find we can match your tricks every time!

(*Sound of the* GUARD *coming suddenly ceases close outside the door up* R.)

SERGEANT OF THE GUARD. (*close outside door up* R. C.) What's the matter here! Let us in!

THORNE. (*loud, incisive voice. Still facing front*) Break down the door Sergeant! Break it down! (*as he calls begins to back up stage toward up* R. C.)

(*Officers and men outside at once begin to smash in the door with the butts of their muskets.*)

ARRELSFORD. (L. C. *surprised*) What are you saying about it!

THORNE. (*up* R. C.) You want 'im in here, don't you!

(ARRELSFORD *moves up a little as* THORNE *does, and covers him with revolver.*)

ARRELSFORD. (L. C. *through noise of breaking door*) Stand where you are!

(THORNE *has backed up* R. C. *until nearly between* ARRELSFORD *and the door, so that the latter cannot fire on him without hitting others. But he must stand a trifle to right of line the men will take in rushing across to* ARRELSFORD.)

THORNE. (*up* R. C. *facing* ARRELSFORD) Smash in the door! What are you waiting for! Smash it in Sergeant! (*keeps up this call till door breaks down and men rush in—which must be at once.— Door is quickly battered in and* SERGEANT *and men rush on.* THORNE, *continuing without break from last speech, above all the noise, pointing to* ARRELSFORD *with* L. *hand*) Arrest that man! (SERGEANT OF THE GUARD *and six men spring forward past* THORNE *and seize* ARRELSFORD *before he can recover from his astonishment, throwing him nearly down in the first struggle, but pulling him to his feet and holding him fast. Two men throwing their guns to two others—seize* THORNE. *An instant motionless on this.* ARRELSFORD *held fast down* L. THORNE *pointing to him up* R. C. *As soon as quiet* THORNE *moves down* C.) He's got in here with a revolver and he's playing Hell with it!

ARRELSFORD. (L. C.) Sergeant—my orders are—

THORNE. (*at* C. *facing* ARRELSFORD) Damn your orders! You haven't got orders to shoot everybody you see in this office! (ARRELSFORD *makes a sudden effort to break loose*) Get his gun away—he'll hurt himself! (*turns* R. *at once and goes to table* R. C. *putting his coat in better position on back of chair, and then getting things in shape on the table. At*

same time putting cigar back in mouth and smoking.
SERGEANT *and men quick bus. of twisting revolver
out of* ARRELSFORD'S *hands*)

ARRELSFORD. (L. C. *continuing to struggle and
protest*) Listen to me! Arrest him! He's sending
out a false——

SERGEANT OF THE GUARD. (L. C.) Now that'll
do! (*silencing* ARRELSFORD *roughly by hand across
his mouth.—To* THORNE) What's it all about,
Cap'n?

THORNE. (*at table arranging things*) All about!
I haven't got the slightest—(*sudden snatch of cigar
out of mouth with* R. *hand and then to* SERGEANT
as if remembering something) He says he came out
of some office! Sending out dispatches here he began
letting off his gun at me. (*go right on half sotto
voce as he again turns arranging things on table*)
Crazy lunatic!

ARRELSFORD. (*struggling to speak. On cue " gun
at me "*) It's a lie! Let me speak—I'm from the—

SERGEANT OF THE GUARD. (*quietly to avoid laugh*)
Here! That'll do now! (*silencing* ARRELSFORD.
To THORNE) What shall we do with him?

THORNE. (*tossing things into place on table with
one hand*) I don't care a damn—get him out o'
here—that's all I want!

SERGEANT OF THE GUARD. Much hurt, Cap'n?

THORNE. (*carelessly*) Oh no. Did up one hand
a little—I can get along with the other all right.
(*sits at table and begins telegraphing*)

ARRELSFORD. (*struggling desperately*) Stop him!
He's sending a—wait! Ask Miss Varney! She saw
him! Ask her! Ask Miss Varney! (*speaks until
stopped. Wildly—losing all control of himself*)

SERGEANT OF THE GUARD. (*breaking in on
ARRELSFORD) Here! Fall in there. We'll get him
out. (*the guard quickly falls in behind* ARRELSFORD,
who is still struggling) Forward——

(*Enter quickly an* OFFICER *striding in to* C.)

OFFICER. (*loud voice—above the noise*)   Halt!
The General!   (OFFICER *remains up stage standing*
L. *of door* R.)

SERGEANT OF THE GUARD. (*to men quickly*) Halt!
(*men on motion from* SERGEANT *stand back, forming
a double rank behind* ARRELSFORD. *Two men holding him in front rank. All facing to* C. SERGEANT
up L. C.)

(*Enter* MAJOR GENERAL HARRISON RANDOLPH
     striding in at door up R. C. CAROLINE *comes to
     door after the* GENERAL, *and stands just within,
     up* R. C. ARRELSFORD *has been so astonished and
     indignant at his treatment that he can't find his
     voice at first.—*OFFICERS *salute as* GENERAL
     RANDOLPH *comes in.* THORNE *goes on working
     instrument at table down* R. C. *cigar between
     his teeth. He has the dispatch with signature
     pasted on it spread on table before him.*)

GENERAL RANDOLPH. (*comes down* C. *and stops*)
What's all this about refusing to send Miss Mitford's
telegram!   Is it some of your work Arrelsford?

ARRELSFORD. (*breathless, violent, excited*)   General!   They've arrested me   A conspiracy!   A—
(*sees* THORNE *working at telegraph instrument*)
Stop that man—for God's sake stop him before it's
too late!

(CAROLINE *edging gradually up* R. C. *quietly slips
     out at door up* R. C.   *Make this exit unnoticed if
     possible.*)

GENERAL RANDOLPH.   (C.)   Stop him!   What
do you mean?

THORNE. (R. C. *back at table.   Rising quickly so*

as to speak on cue, with salute) He means me sir!
He's got an idea some dispatch I'm sending out is
a trick of the Yankees!

ARRELSFORD. (*excitedly*) it's a conspiracy. He's
an impostor—a—a——

THORNE. Why the man must have gone crazy
General! (THORNE *stands facing* L. *motionless*)

ARRELSFORD. I came here on a case for——

GENERAL RANDOLPH. (*sharply*) Wait! I'll get
at this! (*to* SERGEANT *without turning to him*)
What was he doing?

SERGEANT OF THE GUARD. (*up* L. C. *with salute*)
He was firing on the Cap'n sir.

ARRELSFORD. He was sending out a false order to
weaken our lines at Cemetery Hill and I—ah—(*suddenly recollecting*) Miss Varney! (*looking excitedly about*) She was here—she saw it all!

GENERAL RANDOLPH. (*gruffly*) Miss Varney!

ARRELSFORD. Yes sir!

GENERAL RANDOLPH. The General's daughter?

ARRELSFORD. (*nodding affirmatively with excited eagerness*) Yes sir!

GENERAL RANDOLPH. What was she doing here?

ARRELSFORD. She came to see for herself whether
he was guilty or not!

GENERAL RANDOLPH. Is this some personal matter of yours?

ARRELSFORD. He was a visitor at their house—I
wanted her to know!

GENERAL RANDOLPH. Where is she now? Where
is Miss Varney?

ARRELSFORD. (*looking about excitedly*) She must
be out there on the balcony! Send for her!

GENERAL RANDOLPH. Sergeant! (SERGEANT
steps down L. *of* GENERAL RANDOLPH *and salutes*)
Step out there on the balcony. Present my compliments to Miss Varney and ask her to come in!

(SARGENT *salutes and steps quickly out through middle window on the balcony up* L. *Walks off at*
L. *Re-appears walking back as far as balcony
goes. Turns and re-enters room, coming down*
L. C. *and saluting.*)

SERGEANT OF THE GUARD. (*saluting*)   No one
there sir!

(THORNE *turns and begins to send dispatch, picking
up the forged order with* L. *hand as if sending
from that copy and quickly opening instrument*
A. *and telegraphing with* R. *all on nearly same*
• *motion.*)

ARRELSFORD.   She must be there!   She's in the
next office!   The other window.   Tell him to—(*sees
THORNE working at instrument* A.)   Ah!   (*almost
screaming*)   Stop him!   He's sending it now!
GENERAL RANDOLPH. (*to* THORNE)   One moment
Cap'n!   (THORNE *stops. Salutes. Drops dispatch
in* L. *hand to table. Pause for an instant—all holding their positions.* GENERAL RANDOLPH *after above
pause—to* ARRELSFORD)   What have *you* got to do
with this?
ARRELSFORD.   It's a Department Case!   They assigned it to me!
GENERAL RANDOLPH.   What's a Department Case?
ARRELSFORD.   The whole plot—to send the order—
it's the Yankee Secret Service!   His brother brought
in the signal to-night!

(GENERAL RANDOLPH *looks sharply at* ARRELSFORD.)

THORNE. (*very quiet, matter-of-fact*)   This ought
to go out sir—it's very important.
GENERAL RANDOLPH.   Go ahead with it!

(THORNE *salutes and quickly turns to instrument*
A. *dropping dispatch on table and begins send-*
ing rapidly as he stands before the table, glanc-
ing at the dispatch as he does so as if sending
from it.)

ARRELSFORD. (*seeing what is going on*) No no!
It's a——
GENERAL RANDOLPH. Silence!
ARRELSFORD. (*excitedly*) Do you know what he's
telling them!
GENERAL RANDOLPH. No! Do you?
ARRELSFORD. Yes! If you'll——
GENERAL RANDOLPH. (*to* THORNE) Wait!
(THORNE *stops telegraphing, coming at once to*
salute, military position a step back from table facing
front) Where's that dispatch? (THORNE *goes to*
GENERAL RANDOLPH *and hands him the dispatch.*
Then back a step. GENERAL RANDOLPH *takes the*
dispatch. To ARRELSFORD) What was it? What
has he been telling them? (*looks at dispatch in his*
hand)
ARRELSFORD. (*excitedly*) He began to give an
order to withdraw Marston's Division from its present position!
GENERAL RANDOLPH. That is perfectly correct.
ARRELSFORD. Yes—by that dispatch—but that
dispatch is a forgery! (THORNE *with a look of sur-*
prise turns sharply toward ARRELSFORD) It's an
order to withdraw a whole division from a vital
point! A false order! He wrote it himself!
(THORNE *stands as if astounded*)
GENERAL RANDOLPH. Why should he write it? If
he wanted to send out a false order he could
do it without setting it down on paper, couldn't
he?
ARRELSFORD. Yes—but if any of the operators
came back they'd catch him doing it! With that

order and the Secretary's signature he could go right on! He could even order one of them to send it!

General Randolph. How did he get the Secretary's signature?

Arrelsford. He tore it off from a genuine dispatch! Why General—look at that dispatch in your hand! The Secretary's signature is pasted on! I saw him do it!

Thorne. (R. C.) Why—they often come that way! (*turns away nonchalantly toward front*)

Arrelsford. (L. C.) He's a liar! They never do!

(Thorne *turns indignantly on "liar" and the two men glare at each other a moment.*)

Thorne. (R. C. *recovering himself, after bus. and pause*) General, if you have any doubts about that dispatch send it back to the War Office and have it verified!

(Arrelsford *is so thundertsruck that he starts back a little unable to speak. Stands with his eyes riveted to* Thorne *until cue of telegraph click below.*)

General Randolph. (C. *slowly, his eyes on* Thorne) Quite a good idea! (*brief pause*) Sergeant! (*holding out the dispatch.* Sergeant of the Guard *salutes and waits for orders*) Take this dispatch over to the Secretary's office and—(*sudden loud click of telegraph instrument* A. *on table* R. C. General Randolph *stops—listening. To* Thorne) What's that?

(Arrelsford *looking at the instrument.* Thorne *stands motionless, excepting that he took his eyes off* Arrelsford *and looked front listening on click of instrument.*)

THORNE. (*after slight wait—motionless*)   Adjutant-General Chesney.

GENERAL RANDOLPH. From the front?

THORNE. Yes sir.

GENERAL RANDOLPH. What does he say?

(THORNE *turns and steps to table. Stands eyes front, listening to instrument.*)

THORNE.   His compliments sir—(*Pause—Continued click of instrument*) He asks—(*Pause.—Continued click of instrument*) for the rest—(*Pause—continued click of instrument*) of that dispatch—(*Pause—continued click of instrument. Then stops*) It's of vital importance. (THORNE *stands motionless*)

GENERAL RANDOLPH. (*after very slight pause abruptly turns and hands the dispatch back to* THORNE) Let him have it! (THORNE *hurried salute, takes dispatch—sits at table and begins sending*) .

ARRELSFORD. General—if you——

GENERAL RANDOLPH. (*sharply to* ARRELSFORD) That's enough! We'll have you examined at headquarters! (*hurried steps in corridor outside up* R. *and enter quickly at door up* R. *the* FIRST OPERATOR. *He is breathless and excited*)

ARRELSFORD. (*catching sight of* FIRST OPERATOR *as he comes in*) Ah! Thank God! There's a witness! He was sent away on a forged order! Ask him! Ask him! (*pause.* FIRST OPERATOR *standing up stage* R. C. *looking at others surprised.* THORNE *who goes on with bus. at instrument*)

GENERAL RANDOLPH. (*after instant's pause during which click of instrument is heard*) Wait a moment, Cap'n!

(THORNE *stops telegraphing, sits motionless, hand*

on the key. An instant of dead silence. GEN-
ERAL RANDOLPH *moves up* C. *to speak to* FIRST
OPERATOR.)

GENERAL RANDOLPH. (*up* C. *to* FIRST OPERATOR.
Gruffly) Where did you come from?

FIRST OPERATOR. (*up* R. C. *Not understanding
exactly what is going on. Salutes*) There was
some mistake sir!

(ARRELSFORD *gives gasp of triumph quick on cue.
Brief pause of dead silence.*)

GENERAL RANDOLPH. Mistake eh? Who made
it?

FIRST OPERATOR. I got an order to go to the
President's house, and when I got there the President——!

THORNE. (*rising at telegraph table, on cue
" President's house "*) This delay will be disastrous
sir! Permit me to go on—if there's any mistake we
can rectify it afterwards! (*turns to instrument and
begins sending as he stands before it*)

ARRELSFORD. (*half suppressed cry of remon-
strance*) No!

GENERAL RANDOLPH. (*who has not given heed to
THORNE's speech—to FIRST OPERATOR*) Where did
you get the order?

ARRELSFORD. He's at it again sir!

GENERAL RANDOLPH. (*suddenly sees what
THORNE is doing*) Halt there! (THORNE *stops telegraphing*) What are you doing! I ordered you to
wait!

THORNE. (*turns* L. *to* GENERAL RANDOLPH) I was
sent here to attend to the business of this office and
that business is going on! (*turning again as if to
telegraph*)

GENERAL RANDOLPH. (*coming down* C. *a step.*

His temper rising) It's not going on sir, until I'm ready for it!

THORNE. (*turning back to the* GENERAL. *Loud voice, angrily*) My orders come from the War Department—not from you! This dispatch came in half an hour ago—they're calling for it—and it's my business to send it out! (*turning at end of speech and seizing the key endeavors to rush off the dispatch*)

GENERAL RANDOLPH. Halt! (THORNE *goes on telegraphing.* To SERGEANT OF THE GUARD) Sergeant! (SERGEANT *salutes*) Hold that machine there! (*pointing at telegraph instrument.* SERGEANT OF THE GUARD *and two men spring quickly across to* R. SERGEANT *rushes against* THORNE *with arm across his breast forcing him over to* R. *against chair and table on right—chair a little away from table to emphasize with crash as* THORNE *is flung against it—and holds him there. The two men cross bayonets over instrument and stand motionless. All done quickly, business-like and with as little disturbance as possible. One man back of table* R. C. *another* L. *of table* R. C. GENERAL RANDOLPH *strides down* C. *and speaks across to* THORNE) I'll have you court-martialed for this!

THORNE. (*breaking loose from* SERGEANT *and coming down* R.) You'll answer yourself sir, for delaying a dispatch of vital importance!

GENERAL RANDOLPH. (*sharply*) Do you mean that!

THORNE. I mean that! And I demand that you let me proceed with the business of this office!

GENERAL RANDOLPH. By what authority do you send that dispatch?

THORNE. I refer you to the Department!

GENERAL RANDOLPH. Show me your order for taking charge of this office!

THORNE. I refer you to the Department! (*stands motionless facing across to* L.)

(EDITH *appears at upper window up* L. *coming on from balcony left, and moves a little into room up* L. C. SERGEANT OF THE GUARD *remains at* R. *above table when* THORNE *broke away from him.*)

GENERAL RANDOLPH. By God then I'll go to the Department! (*swings round and striding up* C. *a little way*) Sergeant! (SERGEANT OF THE GUARD *salutes*) Leave your men on guard there and go over to the War Office—my compliments to the Secretary and will he be so good as to——

ARRELSFORD. (*suddenly breaking out on seeing* EDITH *up* L.) Ah! General! (*pointing to* EDITH) Another witness! Miss Varney! She was here! She saw it all!

(THORNE *on* ARRELSFORD'S *mention of another witness glances quickly up* L. *toward* EDITH, *and at once turns front and stands motionless, waiting.* GENERAL RANDOLPH *turns left and sees* EDITH.)

GENERAL RANDOLPH. (*up* C. *on* R. *bluffly touching hat*) Miss Varney! (EDITH *comes forward a little* L. *of* C.) Do you know anything about this?
EDITH. (*speaks in low voice*) About what, sir?
GENERAL RANDOLPH. Mr. Arrelsford here claims that Captain Thorne is acting without authority in this office and that you can testify to that effect.
EDITH. (*very quietly, in low voice*) Mr. Arrelsford is mistaken! He has the highest authority!

(ARRELSFORD *aghast,* GENERAL RANDOLPH *surprised.* THORNE *facing* L. *listening—motionless.*)

GENERAL RANDOLPH. (*after an instant's pause of surprise*) What authority has he?

EDITH. (*drawing the commission used in Act* I, *from her dress*) The authority of the President of the Confederate States of America! (*handing the commission to* GENERAL RANDOLPH. GENERAL RANDOLPH *takes the commission and at once opens and examines it.* EDITH *stands a moment where she was, looking neither at* ARRELSFORD *nor* THORNE, *then slowly retires up and stands back of others out of the way*)

GENERAL RANDOLPH. (*up* C. *Looking at the commission*) What's this! Major's Commission! Assigned to duty on the Signal Corps! In command of the Telegraph Department!

ARRELSFOFRD. (L. C. *breaking out*) That commission—let me explain how she——

GENERAL RANDOLPH. That'll do!—I suppose this is a forgery too?

ARRELSFORD. Let me tell you sir——

GENERAL RANDOLPH. You've told me enough! Sergeant—take him to headquarters!

SERGEANT OF THE GUARD. (*quick salute*) Fall in there! (*motioning men at instrument. Men at instrument hurry across to* L. *and fall into rank*) Forward march!

(SERGEANT *and* GUARD *quickly rush* ARRELSFORD *across to door up* R. *and off.*)

ARRELSFORD. (*resisting and protesting as he is forced across and off at* R.) No! For God's sake, General, listen to me! It's the Yankee Secret Service! Never mind me, but don't let that dispatch go out! He's a damned Yankee Secret Agent! His brother brought in the signal to-night! (*etc.*)

(*Sound of footsteps of the* GUARD *outside dying away down the corridor and of* ARRELSFORD'S *voice protesting and calling for justice. Short pause,*

THORNE *motionless through above looking front.*
GENERAL RANDOLPH, *who crossed to up* L. C. *on
men forcing* ARRELSFORD *off goes down* C. *and
looks across at* THORNE.)

GENERAL RANDOLPH. (*gruffly*) Cap'n Thorne!
(THORNE *comes to straight military position, goes
to the* GENERAL *at* C. *and salutes.* GENERAL L.
gruffly) It's your own fault Cap'n! If you'd
had the sense to mention this before we'd have
been saved a damned lot o' trouble! There's your
commission! (*handing commission to* THORNE.
THORNE *takes it saluting.*—GENERAL *turns to go*)
I can't understand why they have to be so cursed shy
about their Secret Service Orders! (*goes up toward
door up* R. C. *Stops and speaks to* FIRST OPERATOR
who is standing at R. *of door*) Lieutenant! (FIRST
OPERATOR *salutes. Very gruffly*) Take your orders
from Cap'n Thorne! (*turns and goes heavily off at
door up* R. *very much out of temper*)

(FIRST OPERATOR *goes down* R. *and sits at telegraph
table on extreme* R. *Busy with papers. No
noise.* THORNE *stands facing* L. *commission in*
R. *hand, until the* GENERAL *is off. Turns* R.
*glancing round to see that he is gone, and at
once glides to telegraph instrument* A. *and begins
sending with* R. *hand—still holding commission
in it.* EDITH *comes quickly down to* THORNE
R. C.)

EDITH. (*at* L. *upper corner of table—very near*
THORNE) Cap'n Thorne! (THORNE *stops tele-
graphing and turns quickly to her—hand still on key.
She goes on in low voice, hurried—breathless*) That
gives you authority—long enough to escape from
Richmond!

THORNE. Escape? Impossible! (*Seizes key and
begins to send*)

EDITH. Oh! You wouldn't do it now! (THORNE *turns and looks at her. Stopping bus. of sending*)

EDITH. I brought it—to save your life! I didn't think you'd use it—for anything else! Oh—you wouldn't!

(THORNE *stands looking at her. Sudden sharp call from instrument* A. *turns him back to it.* EDITH *looks at him—covers her face and moans, at same time turning away* L. *She moves up to the door up* R. *and goes out.* THORNE *stands in a desperate struggle with himself as instrument* A. *is clicking off the same signal that he made when calling up the front. He almost seizes the key—then resists—and finally, with a bang of right fist on the table, turns and strides up* L. C. *the Commission crushed in his* R. *hand.*)

FIRST OPERATOR. (*who has been listening to calls of instrument on table* R. C. *rising as* THORNE *comes to a stand up* L. C.) They're calling for that dispatch sir! What shall I do?

THORNE. (*turning quickly*) Send it!

(FIRST OPERATOR *drops into seat at table* R. C. *and begins sending.*)

Note:—He arranges dispatch at L. *of table for* THORNE *to seize.*

(THORNE *stands motionless on the order an instant. As* OPERATOR *begins to send he turns round a little up to* R. *slowly and painfully,* R. *arm up across eyes in a struggle with himself. Suddenly he breaks away and dashes toward table* R. C.)

THORNE. No no—stop! (*seizes the dispatch*

from the table in his R. *hand which still has the
commission crumpled in it*) I won't do it! I won't
do it! (FIRST OPERATOR *rises in surprise on* THORNE
seizing the dispatch, and stands facing him. THORNE
points at instrument unsteadily) Revoke the order!
It was a mistake! I refuse to act under this commission! (*throwing the papers in his* R. *hand down
on the floor and standing* C. *slightly turned away to*
L.)

CURTAIN

*Time of playing—30 minutes.
Wait between* ACTS III *and* IV—*eight minutes.*

ACT IV

ELEVEN O'CLOCK

(SCENE:—*drawing room at* GENERAL VARNEY'S.
This is the same set as in ACTS I *and* II. *The
furniture is somewhat disordered as if left as
it was after the disturbances at the close of the
second act.* 'Couch up R. *where* ARRELSFORD *put
it end of Act* II. *Nothing is broken or upset.
Half light on in room. Lamps lighted but not
strong on. See that portieres on window down*
R. *are closed. Thunder of distant cannonading
and sounds of volleys of musketry and exploding
shells on very strong at times during this act.
Quivering and rather subdued flashes of light—
as the artillery is some miles distant—shown at
windows* R. *on cues. Violent and hurried ringing of church bells in distant parts of the city—
deep, low tones booming out like a fire bell.
Sounds of hurried passing in the street outside,
of bodies of soldiers—artillery—cavalry, etc. on*

*cues, with many horse-hoof and rattling gun car-
riage and chain effects—shouting to horses—
orders, bugle calls, etc., etc.)*

NOTE:—*This thunder of cannonading, shelling
fortifications, musketry, flashes, etc., must be
kept up during the act, coming in now and then
where it will not interfere with dialogue, and so
arranged that the idea of a desperate attack will
not be lost. Possible places for this effect will
be marked thus in the manuscript—(XXX)*

*(At rise of curtain, thunder of artillery and
flashes of light now and then. Ringing of
church and fire bells in distance.)*

*(CAROLINE is discovered in window up R. shrink-
ing back against a curtain and looking over
toward window up R. She starts toward window after a moment, but shrinks back at a blind-
ing flash.)*

(XXX)

*(Enter MRS. VARNEY coming hurriedly down the
stairs from up L. and in at door.)*

MRS. VARNEY. Caroline! (CAROLINE *goes to her.
Takes CAROLINE forward a little C.)* Tell me what
happened? She won't speak! Where has she been?
Where was it?
CAROLINE. *(frightened)* It was at the telegraph
office!
MRS. VARNEY. What did she do? What hap-
pened? Try to tell!

*(Flashes—cannonading—bells, etc., kept up strong.
Effect of passing artillery begins in the distance very pp.)*

CAROLINE. Ah don't know! Ah was afraid and ran out! (*alarm bell very strong*) It's the alarm bell, Mrs. Varney—to call out the reserves!

MRS. VARNEY. Yes—yes! (*a glance of anxiety toward windows right*) They're making a terrible attack to-night. Lieutenant Maxwell was right! That quiet spell was the signal! (*artillery effect louder*)

(CAROLINE *goes to window up* R.)

CAROLINE. (*turning to* MRS. VARNEY *and speaking above noise, which is not yet on full*) It's another regiment of artillery goin' by! They're sendin' 'em all over to Cemetery Hill! That's where the fighting is! Cemetery Hill! (*effect on loud*)

(CAROLINE *watches from window.* MRS. VARNEY *from up* R. C. MRS. VARNEY *crosses over left and rings bell. As effect dies away* MARTHA *enters up left from door* R. *of stairs.*)

MRS. VARNEY. Go up and stay with Miss Edith till I come. Don't leave her a moment! (MARTHA *turns and hurries up the stairway and exits up* L. *Alarm bell and cannon on strong*) Shut the curtains Caroline! (*comes* C. *up a little*)

(CAROLINE *closes the window curtains at right.*)

CAROLINE. Ah'm afraid they're goin' to have a right bad time to-night! (*going to* MRS. VARNEY C.)

MRS. VARNEY. (C. L.) Indeed I'm afraid so! Now try to think dear, who was at the telegraph office? Can't you tell me something?

CAROLINE. (C. R. *shaking her head*) No—only— they arrested Mr. Arrelsford!

MRS. VARNEY. Mr. Arrelsford! Why you don't mean that!

CAROLINE. Yes Ah do! An' General Randolph—
he came—Ah went an' brought him there—an' oh—
he was in a frightful temper!

MRS. VARNEY. And Edith—now you can tell me—
what—what did she do?

CAROLINE. Ah can't Mrs. Varney. Ah don't
know! Ah just waited for her outside—an' when she
came out she couldn't speak—an' then we hurried
home! That's all Ah know, Mrs. Varney—truly!

(*Loud ringing of door bell in another part of the
house.* CAROLINE *and* MRS. VARNEY *turn toward door up L. Noise of heavy steps outside
left and* ARRELSFORD *almost immediately strides
into the room, followed by two privates, who
stand at the door.*)

(CAROLINE *steps back up stage a little as* ARRELSFORD
enters, and MRS. VARNEY *faces him.*)

(XXX)

ARRELSFORD. (L. C. *roughly, as he advances on*
MRS. VARNEY) Is your daughter in the house?

MRS. VARNEY. (C. *after a second's pause*) Yes!

(XXX)

ARRELSFORD. I'll see her if you please!

MRS. VARNEY. I don't know that she'll care to
receive you at present.

ARRELSFORD. What she cares to do at present is of
small consequence! Shall I go up to her room with
these men or will you have her come down?

MRS. VARNEY. Neither one nor the other until
I know your business.

(*Effect of passing cavalry and artillery—strong.*)

ARRELSFORD. (L. C. *excitedly*) My business! I've

got a few questions to ask! Listen to that! (XXX *on strong*) Now you know what "Attack To-night Plan Three" means!

MRS. VARNEY. (C. *change of manner. Surprise*) Is that—the attack!

ARRELSFORD. That's the attack Madam! They're breaking through our lines at Cemetery Hill! That was PLAN THREE! We're rushing over the reserves but they may not get there in time!

(XXX).

(CAROLINE *has crossed at back to* L. *door as if going out, but waits to see what happens.*)

MRS. VARNEY. What has my daughter to do with this?

ARRELSFORD. Do with it! She did it!

MRS. VARNEY. (*astonished*) What!

(*Noise of passing Cavalry Officer going by singly.*)

ARRELSFORD. We had him in his own trap—under arrest—the telegraph under guard—when she brought in that commission!

MRS. VARNEY. (*horrified*) You don't mean she—

ARRELSFORD. Yes—that's it! She put the game in his hands. He got the wires! His cursed dispatch went through. As soon as I got to headquarters they saw the trick! They rushed the guard back— the scoundrel had got away! But we're after him hot, an' if she knows where he is—(*about to turn to and go toward door up* L.) I'll get it out of her!

(XXX)

MRS. VARNEY. You don't suppose my daughter would—(*interrupted*)

ARRELSFORD. (*breaking in on " suppose "*)   I suppose anything!

MRS. VARNEY.   I'll not believe it!

ARRELSFORD.   We can't stop for what you believe! (*as if to go* L. *to stairs*)

(*Stop alarm bells.*)

MRS. VARNEY.   Let me speak to her!

(*Passing cavalry effect has died away by this time.*)

ARRELSFORD.   I'll see her myself!   (*going up* L.)

(CAROLINE *has stepped quietly down so that as* AR-
     RELSFORD *turns to go toward stairway she con-
     fronts him.*)

CAROLINE. (*up* L. C. *between* ARRELSFORD *and
door. Almost on cue of his last speech*)   Where is
your order for this?

ARRELSFORD. (L. C. *after instant's surprise*)   I've
got a word or two to say to you—after I've been
upstairs!

CAROLINE.   Show me your order for going upstairs!

ARRELSFORD.   Department business—I don't require an order!

CAROLINE. (*shaking head*)   Oh, you've made a
mistake about that!   This is a private house!   It
isn't the telegraph office!   If you want to go up any
stairs or see anybody about anything you'll have to
bring an order!   Ah don't know much—but Ah know
enough for that!   (*exit upstairs*)

(XXX *light*)

ARRELSFORD. (*after pause, turns sharply to* MRS.
VARNEY, *who is* R. C.)   Am I to understand Madam,
that you—(*break, interrupted by noise of bell and
steps outside*)

(Loud ringing of door bell in distant part of house, following almost immediately after by the sound of door outside L. *and tramp of many feet in the hallway.)*

(XXX *cavalry effect begins again*)

(ARRELSFORD *and* MRS. VARNEY *turn.*)

(Enter striding on quickly a Sergeant and four men. Men are halted near L. OFFICER *advances to* MRS. VARNEY. ARRELSFORD *steps back a little up* C.)

SERGEANT. (C. *touching his cap roughly*)　Are you the lady that lives here, ma'am?

MRS. VARNEY. (R. C.)　I am Mrs. Varney!

SERGEANT. (C. *interrupting*)　I've got an order to search the house!　(*showing* MRS. VARNEY *the order*)

ARRELSFORD.　Just in time!　(*coming down* L. C.) I'll go through the house if you please!

SERGEANT. (*shortly*)　You can't go through on this order—it was issued to me!

MRS. VARNEY.　You were sent here to——

SERGEANT.　Yes ma'am!　Sorry to trouble you but we'll have to be quick about it!　If we don't get him here we've got to follow down Franklin Street—he's over this way somewhere!　(*turns* L. *about to give orders to men*)

MRS. VARNEY.　Who?　Who is it you——

SERGEANT. (L. C. *up. Hurriedly*)　Man named Thorne—Cap'n of Artillery—that's what he went by! (*turns to his men*)　Here—this way!　That room in there!　(*indicating room up* C.)　Two of you outside!　(*pointing to windows*)　Cut off those windows.

(Two men run into room up C. *and two off at win-*

dows R. *as indicated, throwing open curtains and windows as they do so.* MRS. VARNEY *stands aside* R. C. SERGEANT *glances quickly round the room—pushing desk out and looking behind it, etc. Keep up cavalry effects and flashes during business. Artillery strong during this. These effects distant—as if going down another street several blocks away. During bus.* ARRELSFORD *goes to door* L. *and gives an order to his men. Then he exits door left. Men who came with* ARRELSFORD *exit after him.*)

(XXX)

(*The two men who went off at door up* C. *to search, re-enter shoving the old negro* JONAS *roughly into the room. He is torn and dirty and shows signs of rough handling. They force him down* C. *a little way and he stands crouching.*)

SERGEANT. (R. C. *to men*) Where did you get that?

PRIVATE. (C.) Hiding in a closet sir.

SERGEANT. (*going* C. *To* JONAS) What are you doing in there? If you don't answer me we'll kick the life out of you! (*short pause. To* MRS. VARNEY) Belongs to you Ah reckon?

MRS. VARNEY. (R. *a little*) Yes—but they want him for carrying a message——

SERGEANT. (*interrupting*) Well if they want him they can get him—we're looking for someone else! (*motions to men*) Throw him back in there! (*men shove* JONAS *off at door up* C. *Other men re-enter from windows at right*) Here—this room! Be quick now! Cover that door! (*two men have quick business of searching room down* R. *and* L. *The other two men stand on guard door up* L.) Sorry to disturb you ma'am! (*bell rings off* L.)

MRS. VARNEY. Do what you please—I have nothing to conceal! (*sound of door outside up* L.)

(XXX)

(*Voice of* ORDERLY *calling outside up* L.)

.ORDERLY. (*outside door up* L.) Here! Lend a hand will you!
(*Two men at door up left exit at left to help someone outside.*) (*Enter the* ORDERLY *who took* WILFRED *away in Act II. coming on hurriedly at door up left. Stands just below door—a few steps into room He is splashed with foam and mud from hard riding. He sees* SERGEANT *and salutes*) (SERGEANT *salutes* ORDERLY *and goes over, looking out of window up* R. MRS. VARNEY *upon seeing the* ORDERLY *gives a cry of alarm*)

ORDERLY. Ah've brought back the boy ma'am!

MRS. VARNEY. (R. C. *starting forward*) Oh! What do you—(*breathless*) What——

ORDERLY. We never got out there at all! The Yankees made a raid down at Mechanicsville not three miles out! The Home Guard was goin' by on the dead run to head 'em off an' before I knew it he was in with 'em riding like mad! There was a bit of a skirmish an' he got a clip across the neck—nothing at all ma'am—he rode back all the way an'—— (*Cavalry effects die away gradually*)

MRS. VARNEY. Oh—he's hurt—he's hurt!

ORDERLY. Nothing bad ma'am—don't upset yourself.

MRS. VARNEY. (*starts toward the door*) Where did you—(*stops on seeing* WILFRED) (*enter* WILFRED *at door left supported by two of the* MEN. *He is pale and has a bandage about neck.* MRS. VARNEY *after the slight pause on his entrance goes to him at once*)

MRS. VARNEY. (*going to* WILFRED) Oh Wilfred!

WILFRED. (*motioning* MRS. VARNEY *off*) It's all right—you don't understand! (*Tries to free himself from the man who is supporting him*) What do you want to hold me like that for? (*Frees himself and walks toward* C. *a few steps a little unsteadily but not too much so*)—You see—I can walk all right! (MRS. VARNEY *comes down anxiously on his right and holds him*) (WILFRED *turns and sees his mother and takes her hand with an effort to do it in as casual a manner as possible*) How-dy-do Mother!—Didn't expect me back so soon, did you?—Tell you how it was—(*turns and sees* ORDERLY. *To* ORDERLY) Don't you go away now—Ah'm going back with you —just wait till I rest about a minute. See here! They're ringing the bells to call out the reserves! (*Starting weakly toward door* L.) Ah'll go right now!

(XXX)

MRS. VARNEY. (*gently holding him back*) No no Wilfred—not now!

(NOTE: WILFRED *must get well over to* R. C. *when he speaks to* MRS. VARNEY, *and not move back to left more than a step or two, in order to be near lounge.*)

(XXX *louder*)

WILFRED. (*weakly*) Not now!—You hear that— you hear those bells—and tell me—not now!—I— (*sways a little*) I—(MRS. VARNEY *gives a cry of alarm seeing* WILFRED *is going to faint*)

SERGEANT. (*quick undertone to* MEN) Stand by there! (WILFRED *faints.* MRS. VARNEY *supports him, but almost immediately the* TWO MEN *come to her assistance.* SERGEANT *and* TWO MEN *push lounge*

forward down R. C. *and they quickly lay him on it,
head to the* R. MRS. VARNEY *goes to head of couch,
and holds* WILFRED'S *head as they lay him down*)

(*Cannonading gradually ceases.*)

SERGEANT. (*to one of the men*) Find some water
will you? (*to* MRS. VARNEY) Put his head down
ma'am—he'll be all right in a minute!

(*A* PRIVATE *hurries off at door up* L. *on order to get
water.* SERGEANT *gets chair from up* C. *puts it
back of couch.* MRS. VARNEY *goes back of couch,
attending to* WILFRED. PRIVATE *re-enters with
basin of water and gives it to* MRS. VARNEY)

OFFICER. (*to* MEN) This way now!

(MEN *move quickly to door up left.* OFFICER *gives
quick directions to* MEN *at door up* L. *All exit.
One or two go* R. OFFICER *with most of men
are seen going up the stairway.* ORDERLY *is left
standing* L. *a little below door, exactly as he was.*
MRS. VARNEY *kneeling back of* WILFRED *and
bathing his head tenderly—using her handkerchief*)

ORDERLY. (*after brief pause*) If there ain't any-
anything else ma'am, Ah'd better report back.
MRS. VARNEY. Yes—don't wait!—The wound is
dressed isn't it?
ORDERLY. Yes'm. I took him to the Winder Hospital—they said he'd be on his feet in a day or two—
but he wants to keep quiet a bit.
MRS. VARNEY. Tell the General just how it happened!
ORDERLY. (*touching cap*) Very well ma'am.
(*exit at door up* L.)

(Short pause. MRS. VARNEY *gently bathing* WIL-
FRED'S *head and wrists)* *(Alarm bells die away
excepting one which continues to ring in muffled
tones)* *(*CAROLINE *appears coming down the
stairway absent-mindedly, stopping when part
way down. Sees somebody in the room. Looks
more intently Suddenly runs down the rest of
the way and into the room at door up* L. *stopping dead when a little way in and looking at
what is going on.* MRS. VARNEY *does not see
her at first—*CAROLINE *stands motionless—face
very white.* MRS. VARNEY *after a moment's
pause for above, sees* CAROLINE*)*

(XXX)

MRS. VARNEY. *(rising quickly)* Caroline dear!
(goes to CAROLINE C.*)* It's *nothing!* *(holds* CARO-
LINE, *though the girl seems not to know it, her face
expressionless and her eyes fixed on* WILFRED*)* He's
hardly hurt at all! There—there—don't you faint
too, dear!

CAROLINE. *(very low voice)* Ah'm not going to
faint! *(sees the handkerchief in* MRS. VARNEY'S
hand) Let me—*(takes handkerchief and goes across
toward* WILFRED, *toward front of couch. Turns to*
MRS. VARNEY*)*—Ah can take care of him. Ah
don't need anybody here at all! *(goes toward* WIL-
FRED*)*

MRS. VARNEY. But Caroline——

CAROLINE. *(still with a strange quiet. Looks
calmly at* MRS. VARNEY*)* Mrs. Varney—there's a
heap o' soldiers goin' round upstairs—lookin' in all
the rooms. Ah reckon you'd better go an' attend to
'em.

MRS. VARNEY. Yes yes—I must go a moment!
(going up toward door up L. *stops and turns to*
CAROLINE*)* You know what to do?

CAROLINE. Oh yes! (*dropping down on the floor beside* WILFRED *in front of couch*)

MRS. VARNEY. Bathe his forehead—he isn't badly hurt!—I won't be long! (*exit hurriedly up* L. *closing the portieres or curtains together after her*)

(CAROLINE *on her knees close to* WILFRED, *tenderly bathing his forehead and smoothing his hair*)
(WILFRED *soon begins to show signs of revival.*)

CAROLNE. (*speaking to* WILFRED *in low tone as he revives. Not a continued speech, but with pauses—business, etc.*) Wilfred dear!—Wilfred! You're not hurt much are you?—Oh no—you're not! There there!—You'll feel better in just a minute!—Yes—just a minute! (*etc.*)

WILFRED. (*weakly. Before he realizes what has happened*) Is there—are you—(*looks round with wide open eyes*)

CAROLINE. Oh Wilfred—don't you know me?

WILFRED. (*looks at her*) What are you talking about—of course Ah know you!—Say—what am I doing anyhow—taking a bath?

CAROLINE. No no!—You see Wilfred—you just fainted a little an'——

WILFRED. Fainted! (CAROLINE *nods*) I fainted! (*A weak attempt to rise. Begins to remember*) Oh —(*sinks back weakly*)—Yes of course!—Ah was in a fight with the Yanks—an' got knocked—(*begins to remember that he was wounded. He thinks about it a moment, then looks strangely at* CAROLINE)

CAROLINE. (*after looking at* WILFRED *in silence*) Oh, what is it?

WILFRED. Ah'll tell you one thing right yere! Ah'm not going to load you up with a cripple! Not much!

CAROLINE. Cripple!

WILFRED. Ah reckon Ah've got an arm knocked off haven't I?

CAROLINE. (*quickly*) No no! You haven't Wilfred! (*shaking head emphatically*) They're both on all right!

WILFRED. (*after thinking a moment*) Maybe I had a hand shot away?

CAROLINE. Oh—not a single one!

WILFRED. Are my—are my ears on all right?

CAROLINE. (*looks on both sides of his head*) Oh yes! You needn't trouble about them a minute! (WILFRED *thinks a moment Then turns his eyes slowly upon her*)

WILFRED. How many legs have Ah got left?

CAROLINE. (*looks to see*) All of 'em—Every one!

(*Last alarm bell ceases.*)

WILFRED. (*after pause*) Then—if there's enough of me left to—to amount to anything—(*looks in* CAROLINE'S *face a moment*) you'll take charge of it just the same?—How about that?

CAROLINE. (*after pause*) That's all right too! (CAROLINE *suddenly buries face on his shoulder*) (WILFRED *gets hold of her hand and kisses it*) (*Suddenly raising head and looking at him*) Ah tried to send you a telegram—an' they wouldn't let me!

WILFRED. Did you? (CAROLINE *nods*) What did you say in it? (*pause*) Tell me what you said!

CAROLINE. It was something nice! (*looks away*)

WILFRED. It was, eh? (CAROLINE *nods with her head turned away from him*) (WILFRED *reaches up and turns her head toward him again*) You're sure it was something nice!

CAROLINE. Well Ah wouldn't have gone to work an' telegraphed if it was something *bad* would Ah?

WILFRED. Well if it was good, why didn't you send it?

CAROLINE. Goodness gracious! How could Ah when they wouldn't let me!

WILFRED. Wouldn't let you!

CAROLINE. Ah should think not! (*moves back for* WILFRED'*s business of getting up*) Oh they had a dreadful time at the telegraph office!

WILFRED. Telegraph office. (*tries to recollect*) Telegr—were you there when—(*raising himself*)

(*alarm bell begins to ring again.*)

(XXX)

(CAROLINE *moves back a little frightened—without getting up—watching him.* WILFRED *suddenly tries to get up*) That was it!—They told me at the hospital! (*attempts to rise*)

(XXX)

CAROLINE. (*rising. Trying to prevent him*) Oh, you mustn't!

WILFRED. (*gets partly on his feet and pushes* CAROLINE *away with one hand, holding to the chair near the desk* R. 1 *for support with the other*) He gets hold of our Department Telegraph—sends out a false order—weakens our defense at Cemetery Hill —an' they're down on us in a minute! An' she gave it to him! The Commission!—My sister Edith!

(XXX)

CAROLINE. (L. *of* WILFRED) Oh you don't know —(*interrupted*)

WILFRED. (*imperiously*) Ah know this—if the General was here he'd see her! The General isn't here—Ah'll attend to it!

(XXX)

(WILFRED *begins to feel a dizziness and holds on to*

desk for support. CAROLINE *starts toward him*
in alarm. He braces himself erect again with
an effort and motions her off.—She stops.)

WILFRED. (*after bus.—Weakly but with clear
voice, and commandingly*) Send her to me!
(CAROLINE *stands almost frightened with her eyes
upon him*)

(*Enter* MRS. VARNEY *at door up* L. CAROLINE *hurries toward* MRS. VARNEY *in a frightened way—
glancing back at* WILFRED.)

CAROLINE. He wants to see Edith!
MRS. VARNEY. (*going toward* WILFRED) Not
now Wilfred—you're too weak and ill!

(CAROLINE *remains up* C.)

WILFRED. (R.) Tell her to come here!
MRS. VARNEY. (L. *of* WILFRED) It won't do any
good—she won't speak!
WILFRED. Ah don't want her to speak—Ah'm
going to speak to her!
MRS. VARNEY. Some other time!
WILFRED. (*leaves the chair that he held to and
moves toward door up* L. *as if to pass his mother and*
CAROLINE) If you won't send her to me—Ah'll——
MRS. VARNEY. (*stopping him*) There there! If
you insist I'll call her!
WILFRED. Ah insist!

(XXX)

MRS. VARNEY. (*turns toward door and goes a few
steps, crossing* CAROLINE. *Stops. Turns back to*
CAROLINE) Stay with him, dear!
WILFRED. (*weak voice but commandingly*) Ah'll
see her alone!

(MRS. VARNEY *looks at him an instant. Sees that he means what he says. Motions* CAROLINE *to come.* CAROLINE *looks at* WILFRED *a moment, then turns and slowly goes to door up* L. *where* MRS. VARNEY *is waiting for her, looks sadly back at* WILFRED *again, and then they both go off at door up* L.)

(XXX)

(WILFRED *stands motionless an instant down* R. C. *as he was when the two ladies left the room. Noise of approaching men—low shouts —steps on gravel, etc., outside up* R., *begins in distance. On this* WILFRED *turns and moves up* C. *looking off to right. Then goes behind thickness of door up* C. *but does not open the door.*)

(XXX)

(*Alarm bell ceases. Low sound of distant voices and the tramp of hurrying feet quickly growing louder and louder outside right. When it is on strong,* THORNE *appears springing over balustrade of veranda above window up* R. *and instantly runs forward into the room—knocking over pedestal and vase at* R. *but quickly back against wall or curtains at right so that he will not be seen. He stands there panting—face pale—eyes hunted and desperate. His left hand is bandaged roughly. He has no hat, or coat, hair is disheveled, shoes dusty, trousers and shirt torn and soiled. As the noise of his pursuers dies away he turns into the room and makes a rapid start across toward* L. *Looking quickly about as if searching for someone.*)

(WILFRED—*who has been watching him from up* C.

darts down C. *as* THORNE *goes across and comes
down right of him catching hold of him by right
arm and shoulder.*)

WILFRED. (*on* THORNE'S R. *near* C. *Seizing hold
of* THORNE'S *right arm and shoulder as* THORNE
passes him) Halt! You're under arrest!

THORNE. (*with a quick glance back at* WILFRED)
Wait a minute! (*shaking loose from* WILFRED *and
turning up* L. C.) Wait a minute an' I'll go with
you! (*going up* L., *looking this way and that*)

WILFRED. (*a step toward* THORNE *as if to follow*) Halt I say. You're my prisoner!

THORNE. (*turning and going quickly down to*
WILFRED) All right—prisoner—anything you like!
(*drawing revolver from right hip pocket and pushing it into his hands*) Take this—shoot the life out
of me—but let me see my brother first!

WILFRED. (*taking the revolver*) Your brother!

THORNE. (*nods—breathless*) One look in his
face—that's all!

WILFRED. Where is he?

THORNE. (L. *of* C. *a little. Quick glance about.
Points toward the door up* C.) Maybe they took him
in there! (*striding up* C. *toward door as he speaks*)

WILFRED. (R. *of* C. *a little. Springing up and
covering* THORNE *with revolver*) What is he doing?

THORNE. (*facing* WILFRED *half way up* C.) Ha!

WILFRED. (*still covering* THORNE) What's he
doing in there?

THORNE. Nothing! . . . He's dead! (*stands
motionless facing* R.)

(WILFRED *looks at* THORNE *a moment. Then begins
to back slowly up to door up* C., *keeping eyes on*
THORNE *and revolver ready but not aimed.—
Opens door up* C. *Quick look into the room.
Faces* THORNE *again.*)

WILFRED. It's a lie!

THORNE. (*turning up toward* WILFRED) What!

WILFRED. There's no one there!—It's another trick of yours! (*starts toward window up* R.) Call in the Guard! Call the Guard! Captain Thorne is here in the house!

(WILFRED *exits at window* R. *calling the* GUARD. *His voice is heard outside* R., *becoming more and more distant.*)

(THORNE *stands a moment until* WILFRED *is off then springs to the door up* C.—*opens it and looks into the room, going part way off at the door. He glances this way and that within room then attitude of failure—left hand dropping from frame of door to his side as he comes to erect position. Right hand retaining hold of knob of door, which he pushed open.*)

(On THORNE *standing erect,* EDITH *enters through the portieres of the door up* L.—*expecting to find* WILFRED. *She stands just within the doorway to the* L. *of it.*)

(THORNE *turns and comes out of room up* C., *closing the door as he does so. Turning away from the door—right hand still on the knob—he sees* EDITH *and stops motionless facing her.*)

THORNE. (*going to* EDITH *up* L. C.) You wouldn't tell me would you! He was shot in this room—an hour ago—my brother Harry!—I'd like one look in his dead face before they send me the same way! Can't you tell me that much Miss Varney? Is he in the house. (EDITH *looks in his face an instant motionless—then turns and moves slowly down* L. C. *and stands near the table there*)

THORNE. (*turns and moves toward window up* R.) (*A sudden burst of shouts and calls outside up* R. *in distance on* THORNE'S *turning away to* R. *as if* WILFRED *had reached a posse of the Guard*) (*Turning near* C.—*a flash of distant artillery on him from outside up* R.) Ha ha—they're on the scent you see!—They'll get me in a minute—an' when they do it won't take long to finish me off! (*looks at her*) And as that'll be the last of me—(*moves toward her*) as that'll be the last of me Miss Varney —maybe you'll listen to one thing! We can't all die a soldier's death—in the roar and glory of battle —our friends around us—under the flag we love!— no—not all! Some of us have orders for another kind of work—desperate—dare-devil work—the hazardous schemes of the Secret Service! We fight our battles alone—no comrades to cheer us on—ten thousand to one against us—death at every turn! If we win we escape with our lives—if we lose—dragged out and butchered like dogs—no soldier's grave—not even a trench with the rest of the boys—alone—despised—forgotten! These were my orders Miss Varney—this is the death I die to-night—and I don't want you to think for one minute that I'm ashamed of it—not for one minute!

(*Suddenly shouts and noise of many men running up outside up* R. *and also outside up* L.—THORNE *swings round and walks up* C. *in usual nonchalant manner, and stands up* C. *waiting and faced a little to* R. *of front, leaning on side of door with outstretched right arm*)

(EDITH *moves to left and stands near mantel.*)

(*As shouts become nearer,* THORNE *turns and stands waiting, faced to front. No assumption of bravado. Simply waiting without troubling himself about the affair one way or the other*)

(Enter from both windows on right—bursting open the one down right—and from door up L. a SQUAD *of* CONFEDERATE SOLDIERS *in gray uniforms—not too old and dirty—those on right headed by the* SERGEANT *who searched the house early in this act, and those on left by* CORPORAL, *etc., etc., of former acts.* WILFRED VARNEY *with revolver still in his hand, enters at windows down* R. *in lead of others, coming to* R. C.—*All the available and effective force possible for this. The men themselves must be solid and capable of effective work. Upon no account allow boys in this squad.—They rush on at climax of noise of feet and voices outside, and with a shout of exultation, and stand on charge at each side)*

WILFRED. (R. C. *to* SERGEANT) There's your man Sergeant—I hand him over to you!

SERGEANT. *(Up* R. C.—*Advancing to* THORNE *and putting hand roughly on his shoulder)* Prisoner!

(XXX)

(Enter ARRELSFORD *hurriedly at door up* L.*)*

ARRELSFORD. *(breaking through between men at left and standing* L. C.) Where is he? *(Sees* THORNE) Ah! We've got him have we!

SERGEANT. Young Varney here captured him, sir! *(enter* MRS. VARNEY *up* L. *She goes down left side near* F. P. *and stands looking on)*

ARRELSFORD. *(left of* THORNE) So!—Run down at last! *(*THORNE *pays no attention to* ARRELSFORD. —He merely waits for the end of the disturbance)* Now you'll find out what it costs to play your little game with our Government Telegraph Lines! *(*THORNE *does not even listen.—*ARRELSFORD *turns to* SERGEANT) Don't waste any time! Take him down the street and shoot him full of lead!—Out

with him! (*going down* L. C. *on last of speech*)
(*Low shouts of approval from men, and general
movement as if to start, the* SERGEANT *at same time
shoving* THORNE *a little toward* L.)

SERGEANT. (*gruffly—as he starts. With other
shouts*) Come along!

WILFRED. (*a step toward* C.—*revolver still in
hand*) No! (*on* WILFRED'S '*no*' *all stop. During
the rest of* WILFRED'S *speech* THORNE *turns wearily
away to* L.—*which brings him around facing up stage
a little—near the door up* C.)—Whatever he is—
whatever he's done—he has the right to a trial!
(THORNE *turns suddenly round and looks at* WIL-
FRED)

ARRELSFORD. (*down* L. C.) General Tarleton said
to me, " If you find him shoot him on sight!"

WILFRED. (*down* R. C.) I don't care what General
Tarleton said—I captured the man—he's in this
house—and he's not going out without he's treated
fair! (WILFFED *looks up toward* THORNE. *Their
eyes meet. Then* THORNE *turns away up stage, rest-
ing left hand against* L. *side of door frame*)

ARRELSFORD. (*suddenly. Angrily*) Well—let
him have it!—We'll give him a drum-head, boys—
but it'll be the quickest drum-head ever held on earth!
(*to* SERGEANT) Stack muskets here an' run 'em in
for the court!

SERGEANT. (*stepping a little down* C. *and facing
about—back to audience*) Fall in here! MEN
*break positions each side and run up stage, falling
quickly into a double rank just above* SERGEANT)
Fall in the Prisoner! (MEN *separate* R. & L. *leaving
space at* C. THORNE *steps down into position and
stands*) Stack—arms! (*front rank men stack.—
Rear rank men pass pieces forward. Front rank
men lay them on stacks.—Turning right to* MRS.
VARNEY *and touching cap*) Where shall we find a
vacant room, ma'am?

MRS. VARNEY. At the head of the stairs—there's none on this floor.

SERGEANT. (*turning up to men*) Escort—left face! (*men left face*—THORNE *obeying the order with them*) Forward—march!—File left! (*etc.*)

(SOLDIERS *with* THORNE *march rapidly out of the room at door up* L. *and disappear up the stairway outside up* L. *The* SERGEANT *exits up* L. *after men.*)

(ARRELSFORD *exits after men up* L. *following them closely up the stairway and off* L. WILFRED *goes off and up the stairway with some effort, following the* SERGEANT. MRS. VARNEY *exits at door up left and off to left.*)

NOTE:—*The foregoing scene to be played very rapidly and at high tension. The rush of men on— the capture—*THORNE'S *cool nonchalance—*EDITH *motionless down left. The few words and the hurried exit to drum-head the prisoner—all a sweep of sudden vengeance; with the lurid flashes seen at windows* R. *and the sullen roar of cannon in distance.*

(XXX)

(EDITH *turns and crosses slowly to window at right. Pauses a moment. Flashes of light from distant cannonading on her face. She stands in window right—partly hidden by curtains—looking off.*)

(XXX)

(*The door up* C. *slowly opens a little way so that someone can look through the crack. Soon the old negro* JONAS *enters cautiously—almost crawling on. He looks this way and that and off at door up left and up the stairway. Sud-*

*denly his eyes light on the stacks of muskets.
He goes to the one up* L. C.—*looks about fear-
fully—apprehensively. Hesitates an instant.
During* JONAS' *business—artillery and cavalry
effects on strong. Cannon and musketry fire
in distance—alarm bells on strong—begin as
men go upstairs.*)

(XXX)

(JONAS *makes up his mind to do it. Drops down
on knees by stack of muskets up* L. C.—*snaps
the breech lock of one—without moving it from
the stack—gets out the cartridge, looks at it,
bites it with his teeth and looks at it again.
Bites again and makes motions of getting the
ball off and putting it in his pocket. Puts
cartridge back in the musket, snaps the lock
shut, and moves on to the next. Repeats bus.
of cartridge out, but is much quicker, biting off
the ball at once. Repeats more rapidly and
quickly with another musket, crawling quickly
round the stack. Moves over to stack at* R. C.
Same bus. Make scene as rapidly as possible.)

(*As* JONAS *gets well to work on muskets* EDITH *turns
at window up* R. *and sees him. She stands a
moment motionless—then comes down on right,
and stands looking at him without moving.*
JONAS, *who began after leaving stack* L. C. *at
upper side of stack* R. C. *has worked around down
stage on the stack, and has come to the lower
side.* EDITH *stands near the desk at* R. *and
drops a book upon it on cue to make* JONAS *look
up after the last musket but one.* JONAS *looks
up and sees* EDITH *watching him. He stops.*)

(XXX)

(*Stop loud effects as* JONAS *speaks—but keep up bells and far distant cannon.*)

JONAS. (*after pause. Very low voice*) Dhey's a-goin' ter shoot 'im—shoot 'im down like a dog, Missy—an' Ah couldn't b'ar to see 'em do dat! Ah wouldn't like to see 'im killed—Ah wouldn't like it noways! You won't say nuffin' 'bout dis—fer de sake of ole Jonas what was always so fond o' you— ebber sense ye was a little chile! (*he sees that* EDITH *does not appear angry, and goes on with his work of drawing the bullets out of the last musket*) Ye see —I jiss take away dis yer—an' den dar won't be no harm to 'im what-some-ebber—less'n day loads 'em up agin! (*slowly hobbles to his feet as he speaks*) When dey shoots—an' he jiss draps down, dey'll roll 'im over inter de gutter an' be off like dey was mad! Den Ah can be near by—an'— (*suddenly thinks of something. A look of consternation comes over his face. He speaks in almost whisper*) How's he goin' ter know! Ef he don't drap down dey'll shoot him agin—an dey'll hab bullets in 'em nex' time! (*anxiously glances around an instant*) Dey'll hab bullets in 'em next time! (*looks about. Suddenly to* EDITH) *You* tell 'im! *You* tell him Missy—it's de ony-est way! Tell 'im to drap down! (*supplicatingly*) Do dis fur ole Jonas, honey—do it fur me—an' Ah'll be a slabe to ye ez long ez Ah lib! (*slight pause. Sudden subdued yell outside up left sounding as if from men shut inside a room on the floor above.* JONAS *starts and turns on the yell. Half whisper*) Dey's a-goin' ter kill 'im!

(XXX)

(*Noise of heavy tramp of feet outside* L. *above—doors opening, etc. An indistinct order or two before regular order heard.* JONAS *goes hurriedly up to door up* C.)

SERGEANT.   (*outside* L.—*Above*)—Fall in!—
Right face!—Forward—March!

JONAS. (*at door up* C.)   Oh tell 'im Missy! Tell
'im to drap down for God's sake! (*exit* JONAS *at
door up* C. *carefully closing it after him*)

(XXX)

(EDITH *crosses to* L. C. *and stands waiting, her face
     expressionless, in front of table* L. C.)

(XXX)

(*Enter* WILFRED *up* L. *coming down the stairs.   He
     enters the room coming down* C.   *Enter* CARO-
     LINE *at door up* L. *as* WILFRED *goes down* C.
     *She hurries to him with an anxious glance up
     stairway as she passes.*)

CAROLINE. (C. *on* WILFRED'S L.   *Almost whisper*)
What are they—going to do?
WILFRED. (C.)   Shoot him!
CAROLINE. When?
WILFRED. Now.
CAROLINE. (*low exclamation of pity*)   Oh!

(WILFRED *goes* R. C. *below lounge.   CAROLINE stands
     near him on his* L. *looking on as* SOLDIERS *and
     others enter.*)

(*Enter, coming down stairway up left at back
     the* SERGEANT, *followed by escort of* SOLDIERS.
     They enter room at door or archway up L. *and
     turn* R. *marching to position they were formerly
     in above the stacks of muskets.*)

(*Enter* ARRELSFORD L., *following down the stair-
     way after the escort of* MEN.   *He goes across to*

up R. C. MRS. VARNEY *enters at door up* L. *and goes down* L. *Stands* L.)

SERGEANT. (*Who is at* C. *facing up. When men have come to proper place*) Halt! (MEN *halt*) Left face! (MEN *face front*)

(*Enter* THORNE *up* L. *coming down the stairway, followed by* CORPORAL *with his carbine.* THORNE *comes into position at* L. *of front line of men.* CORPORAL *stands at* L. *of* THORNE.)

SERGEANT. (*after* THORNE *is in position at* L. *of* MEN) Take arms! (MEN *at once take muskets. All very quick*) Carry arms! (*Bus.* MEN *stand in line waiting*) Fall in the Prisoner! (THORNE *walks in front of* MEN *to* C. *and falls into position*) Left face! (THORNE *and* MEN *face to left on order, ready to march out*) Forward— (*interrupted*)
EDITH. (*in front of the table* L. C.) Wait!—(*motion of hand to stop them without looking round*) Who is the officer in command?
SERGEANT. (R. C. *down*) I'm in command, Miss! (*touching cap*)
EDITH. (*to* SERGEANT) I'd like to—speak to the prisoner!
SERGEANT. Sorry Miss, but we haven't got time! (*turning as though to give orders*)
EDITH. (*sudden turn on him and hand out*) Only a word!

(SERGEANT *stops* C. *looking at her—hesitates an instant—turns to* MEN. *Stepping up* L. C.)

SERGEANT. Right face! (MEN *face to front again on order.* THORNE *obeying order with others*) Fall out the prisoner! (THORNE *moves forward one step out of rank and stands motionless*) Now Miss!

WILFRED. (*starting indignantly toward Centre*)
No!

(*Tableau an instant.* SERGEANT *turns in surprise.*)

CAROLINE. (*holding to* WILFRED *and speaking in
a low voice full of feeling*) Oh Wilfred—let her
speak to him—let her say good-bye!

(WILFRED *looks at* CAROLINE *a moment. Then with
    gesture to* SERGEANT *indicates that he may go
    on, and turns away* R. *with* CAROLINE.)

SERGEANT. (*turning to* THORNE) The lady!

(*A brief motionless pause—*THORNE *looking front as
    before. Then he turns slowly and looks at* SER-
    GEANT—SERGEANT *turns and looks meaningly
    toward* EDITH. THORNE *walks down to her,
    stopping close on her right, standing in military
    position, faced, as he walked, a little to* L. *of
    front.*)

(ARRELSFORD *up* R. C. *looking at* EDITH *and* THORNE.
    CAROLINE *with* WILFRED *down* R. C. *gives an
    occasional awed and frightened glance at*
    THORNE *and* EDITH. *All this arranged so that
    there is no movement after the* SERGEANT'S *order
    to " fall out the prisoner."*)

(EDITH, *after slight pause, speaks slowly in almost a
    whisper and as if with an effort, but without
    apparent feeling, and without turning to*
    THORNE.)

EDITH. (*voice for* THORNE *alone to hear.
Slowly. Distinctly. Without inflection. A slight
occasional tremor. Pauses as indicated*) One of

the servants—has taken the musket balls—out of the guns. If you care to fall on the ground when they fire—you may escape with your life!

THORNE. (*after pause. To* EDITH. *Low voice*) Do you wish me to do this?

EDITH. (*Low voice—without turning*) It's nothing to me.

(THORNE, *with slight sudden movement at the cue, turns slowly away to front.—Brief pause. He turns toward her again.*)

THORNE. (*very low voice*) Were you responsible in any way for—(EDITH *shakes her head slightly without looking at him.* THORNE *turns and walks right a step or two to* C.—*Makes turn there and walks up* C. *and turns to* L. *facing the* SERGEANT *a little* R. *of* C. *and out of the way of bayonets in coming business. Saluting*) Sergeant— (*as if making an ordinary military report*) You'd better take a look at your muskets—they've been tampered with.

SERGEANT. (*snatching musket from man nearest him*) What the— (*quickly snaps it open. Cartridge drops to floor.* SERGEANT *picks it up and looks at it*) Here!— (*handing musket back to man. Turns to squad and gives orders quickly as follows: Business on these orders very effective if carried out promptly and with precision*) Squad—ready! (MEN *come in one movement from " carry " to position for loading*) Draw—cartridge! (MEN *draw cartridges. The click and snap of locks and levers ringing out simultaneously along the line*) With ball cartridge—reload! (MEN *quickly reload. Same bus. of rapid click of locks and levers down the line*) Carry—arms! (MEN *come to carry on the instant. Motionless. Eyes front. To* THORNE— *with off-hand salute*) Much obliged sir!

THORNE. (*low voice. Off-hand—as if of no con-*

sequence) That's all right. (*stands facing* L. *waiting for order to fall in.* WILFRED, *after* THORNE'S *warning to officer about muskets, watches him with undisguised admiration*)

WILFRED. (*suddenly walking up to* THORNE) Ah'd like to shake hands with you!

(THORNE *turns and looks at* WILFRED, *who is just below him a little to his right. A smile breaks gradually over his face.*)

THORNE. (*smiling*) Is this for yourself—or your father?

WILFRED. (*earnestly*) For both of us sir! (*putting out his hand a little way—not raising it much*) (THORNE *grasps his hand, they look into each other's faces a moment, let go hands,* WILFRED *turns away to down* R. C. *and goes up back of couch to* CAROLINE. THORNE *looks after* WILFRED *to front an instant—then turns* L.) That's all, Sergeant!

SERGEANT. (*lower voice than before*) Fall in the Prisoner! (THORNE *steps to place in the line and turns front*) Escort—left face! (MEN *with* THORNE *left face*) Forward ma—(*sharp cry of* "Halt! Halt!" *outside up* L., *followed by bang of heavy door outside* L.)

SERGEANT. Halt! (MEN—*who have not started—stand motionless at left face. On seeing the* ORDERLY *approaching—just before he is on*) Right face!

(MEN *with* THORNE *face to front.*)

(*Enter quickly at door up* L. *an* AID—*wearing Lieutenant's uniform.* SERGEANT, *faced front up* L. C. *just forward of his men, salutes.* AID *salutes.*)

SERGEANT. (*low voice to* MEN) Present—arms!

(MEN *Present*) Carry—arms! (MEN *come to carry
again*)

(WILFRED *and* CAROLINE *move quietly around right
end of lounge to* R. C. *above it. Come to position before* AID *speaks.*)

(XXX)

AID. (*standing up* L. C.—*facing* R.) General
Randolph's compliments sir, and he's on the way
with orders!

ARRELSFORD. (*up* R. C.) What orders, Lieutenant?—Anything to do with this case?

AID. (*no salute to* ARRELSFORD) I don't know
what the orders are, sir. He's been with the President.

ARRELSFORD. I sent word to the Department we'd
got the man and were going to drum-head him on the
spot.

AID. Then this must be the case sir. I believe
the General wishes to be present.

ARRELSFORD. Impossible! We've held the court
and I've sent the finding to the Secretary! The messenger is to get his approval and meet us at the
corner of Copley Street.

AID. I have no further orders sir! (*retires up
with quick military movement and turns facing
front. Stands motionless*)

(XXX)

(*Sound of door outside up* L. *and the heavy tread
of the* GENERAL *as he strides across the hall.*)

SERGEANT. (*low voice to* MEN) Present—arms!
(MEN *present*)

(SERGEANT, ORDERLY, ETC., *on salute.*)

(Enter General Randolph *at door up* L., *striding on hurriedly—returning salutes as he crosses to* R. C. *glancing about.)*

(Enter, after General Randolph, *as if he had come with him, the* First Telegraph Operator, *(Lieutenant Foray)* He stands waiting near door, faced front, military position.)*

Sergeant. *(low order to* Men) Carry—arms! *(*Men *come to carry again)*

General Randolph. Ah, Sergeant!—*(going down and across to* R.) Got the prisoner in here have you?

Sergeant. *(saluting)* Just taking him out sir!

General Randolph. (R.) Prison?

Sergeant. No sir! To execute the sentence of the Court!

General Randolph. Had his trial then!

Arrelsford. *(stopping down* R. C. *with a salute)* All done according to regulations, sir! The finding has gone to the Secretary!

General Randolph. (R. *to* Arrelsford) Found guilty I judge?

Arrelsford. Found guilty sir!—No time for hanging now—the court ordered him shot!

General Randolph. What were the grounds for this?

Arrelsford. Conspiracy against our government and the success of our arms by sending a false and misleading dispatch containing forged orders!

General Randolph. Court's been misinformed. The dispatch wasn't sent!

*(*Edith *looks up with sudden breathless exclamation.* Wilfred *turns with surprise. General astonishment.)*

ARRELSFORD. (*recovering*)   Why General—the
dispatch—I saw him——

GENERAL RANDOLPH.   I say the dispatch wasn't
sent! I expected to arrive in time for the trial and
brought Foray here to testify. (*calls to* LIEUTEN-
ANT FORAY *without looking round*)   Lieutenant!

(LIEUTENANT FORAY *comes quickly down* L. C. *facing* GENERAL RANDOLPH.—*Salutes.*)

Did Captain Thorne send out any dispatches after
we left you with him in the office an hour ago?

LIEUTENANT FORAY.   No sir. I was just going
to send one under his order, but he countermanded it.

GENERAL RANDOLPH.   What were his words at the
time?

LIEUTENANT FORAY.   He said he refused to act
under that commission.

(EDITH *turns toward* THORNE *and looks at him
steadfastly.*)

GENERAL RANDOLPH.   That'll do, Lieutenant!
(LIEUTENANT FORAY *salutes and retires up* L.)   In
addition we learn from General Chesney that no
orders were received over the wire—that Marston's
Division was not withdrawn—and that our position
was not weakened in any way. The attack at that
point has been repulsed. It's plain that the Court
has been acting under error. The President is there-
fore compelled to disapprove the finding and it is set
aside.

ARRELSFORD. (C. *With great indignation*)   General Randolph, this case was put in my hands and
I——

GENERAL RANDOLPH. (*interrupting bluffly, but
without temper*)   Well I take it out of your hands!
Report back to the War Office with my compliments!

(ARRELSFORD *turns and starts toward up* L.)

ARRELSFORD. (*after going a few steps turns back
again*) Hadn't I better wait and see—

GENERAL RANDOLPH. No—don't wait to see anything! (ARRELSFORD *looks at* GENERAL RANDOLPH
an instant. Then turns and exits at door up L.
Sound of door outside up L. *closed with force.*
GENERAL RANDOLPH *in front of lounge*)   Sergeant! (SERGEANT *quickly down to* GENERAL RAN-
DOLPH *on salute. Standing on his* L.)   Hold your
men back there. I'll see the prisoner. (SERGEANT
*salutes, turns, marches straight up from where he
is to the right division of the escort so that he is a
little to right of* THORNE *and turns front*)

SERGEANT. Order—arms! (*Squad obeys with
precision*)   Parade—rest! (*Squad obeys order*)
Fall out the Prisoner! (THORNE *steps forward one
step out of the rank and stands*)   The General!
(THORNE *starts down* C. *to go to* GENERAL RANDOLPH.
As THORNE *steps forward on order—" The General "
—to walk down* C. EDITH *starts quickly toward* C.
*and intercepts him about two-thirds of the way down,
on his left.* THORNE *stopped by* EDITH *shows slight
surprise for an instant, but quickly recovers and
looks straight front*)

EDITH. (*to* THORNE *as she meets him. Impulsively. But low voice*)   Oh—why didn't you
tell me!—I thought you sent it! I thought you—

GENERAL RANDOLPH. (*surprised*)   Miss Varney!

EDITH. (*crossing* THORNE *and speaking impetuously to the* GENERAL)   There's nothing against him.
General Randolph!—He didn't send it!—There's
nothing to try him for now!

GENERAL RANDOLPH. You're very much mistaken, Miss Varney. The fact of his being caught
in our lines without his uniform is enough to swing
him off in ten minutes.

(EDITH *moans a little, at same time moving back from* GENERAL *a trifle.*)

GENERAL RANDOLPH. Cap'n Thorne—(THORNE *steps down and faces* GENERAL) or whatever your name may be—the President is fully informed regarding the circumstances of your case, and I needn't say that we look on you as a cursed dangerous character! There isn't any doubt whatever that you'd ought to be exterminated right now!—But considering the damned peculiarity of your behavior—and that you refused for some reason—to send that dispatch when you might have done so, we've decided to keep you out of mischief some other way. The Sergeant will turn you over to Major Whitfield sir! (SERGEANT *up* R. C. *salutes*) You'll be held as a prisoner of war! (*turns and goes* R. *a few steps*)

(EDITH *turns suddenly to* THORNE, *coming down before him as he faces* R.)
EDITH. (*looking in his face*) Oh—that isn't nearly so bad!

(THORNE *holds her hand in his right.*)

THORNE. No?
EDITH. No!—Because—sometime— (*hesitates*)
THORNE. (*his face nearer hers*) Ah—if it's sometime, that's enough!

(*Slight pause.* EDITH *sees* MRS. VARNEY *at* L. *and crosses to her,* THORNE *retaining her hand as she crosses—a step back to let her pass—following her with his eyes—releasing her hand only when he has to.*)

EDITH. Mamma, won't you speak to him?

(MRS. VARNEY *and* EDITH L. *talk quietly.*)

WILFRED. (*suddenly leaving* CAROLINE *up* R. C. *and striding down from behind couch to* THORNE, *extending hand*) I'd like to shake hands with you!
THORNE. (*turning to* WILFRED) What, again? (*taking* WILFRED'S *hand. Under breath as he does so*) All right—go ahead.

(WILFRED, *shaking hands with* THORNE *and crossing him to* L. *as he does so—back to audience, laughing and very happy about it.*)

CAROLINE. (*coming quickly down, pushing* SERGEANT *back out of the way as she goes*) So would I! (*holding out her hand*)

(THORNE *let go* WILFRED'S *hand—now on his left and takes* CAROLINE'S.—WILFRED *a little below on his left*—CAROLINE *level on his right.*)

WILFRED. Don't you be afraid now—it'll be all right! They'll give you a parole and——
CAROLINE. (*breaking in enthusiastically*) A parole! Goodness gracious! Why they'll give you hundreds of 'em! *turning away with funny little comprehensive gesture of both hands on end of her speech*)
GENERAL RANDOLPH. (*gruffly*) One moment if you please! THORNE *turns at once, facing* GENERAL RANDOLPH *near* C. CAROLINE *and* WILFRED *go up* R. C. *to above couch.* EDITH *stands* L. C. MRS. VARNEY *near table* L.) There's only one reason on earth why the President has set aside a certain verdict of death. You held up that false order and made a turn in our favor. We expect you to make the turn complete and enter our service.

(*All motionless—watching the scene.*)

THORNE. (*after instant's pause. Quietly*) Why General—that's impossible!

GENERAL RANDOLPH. (R.) You can give us your answer later!

THORNE. (C.) You have it now!

GENERAL RANDOLPH. You'll be kept in close confinement until you come to our terms!

THORNE. You're making me a prisoner for life!

GENERAL RANDOLPH. You'll see it in another light before many days. And it wouldn't surprise me if Miss Varney had something to do with your change of views!

EDITH. (*coming toward* C.) You're mistaken General Randolph—I think he's perfectly right!

(THORNE *turns to* EDITH *and moves toward her getting her hand in his* R.)

GENERAL RANDOLPH. Very well—we'll see what a little prison life will do. (*a sharp order*) Sergeant! (SERGEANT *comes down* R. C. *and salutes*) Report with the prisoner to Major Whitfield! (*turns away to front*)

(SERGEANT *turns at once to* THORNE.—THORNE *and* EDITH *look in each other's eyes.*)

THORNE. (*low voice to* EDITH) What is it—love and Good-bye?

EDITH. (*almost a whisper*) Oh no—only the first!—And that one every day—every hour—every minute—until we meet again!

THORNE. Until we meet again!

SERGEANT. (R. C. *up*) Fall in the Prisoner!

(THORNE *turns and walks up, quickly taking his place in the Squad.*—EDITH *follows him up a step or two as he goes, stopping a little* L. *of* C.)

SERGEANT. (*quick orders*) Attention! (*Squad*

obeys order)   Carry—arms!   (*Squad obeys order*)
Escort—left—face!   (*Squad with* THORNE—*left face
on the order*)   Forward—march!

(*Escort with* THORNE *marches out at door up* L. *and
off to* L.)

CURTAIN

Time of playing—25 minutes.